The Wish Weaver

By Dash Hoffman

Written by Dash Hoffman

Published by Dash Hoffman at Paris Publishing

Copyright 2017 Dash Hoffman

Other Books By
Dash Hoffman

Mrs. Perivale and the Blue Fire Crystal
The Starling Chronicles
The Lost Boy
Journey Blue
Voyager: The Butterfly Effect
The Zodiac Thief
The Dragon Slayer's Daughter
And more…

Dedications

For Roma and Myra
who have wished for this fairytale

And for all those who wish, whether on stars or coins in
a fountain, on birthday candles or any other hope... may
your best wishes come true.

Table of Contents

Chapter One

A Circle of Friends

Once upon a time, long ago and far away, there was a beautiful wild country where fairytales, dreams, and wishes were real. It was there that the great Kamala mountain range reached its jagged peaks so far up into the heavens that they seemed to nearly touch the stars. Though the universe was too lofty for them, the mighty giants gazed low upon the passing clouds, catching them in the folds of towering trees and in the depths of twisting canyons, and holding them as they wept rain in rivers down the cliffs and mountain walls to the valleys at the feet of the titans.

It was there, between the foothills of the Kamalas and the wide-open fields of the farmlands to the east, that a small village was nestled into gently rolling hills and skirted prettily with a rambling river separating it from the span of pastures. The village of Zorion had been there for as long as anyone in it could remember, and for as long as their greatest grandparents could remember, and perhaps even much longer than that.

Zorion had ambled along quietly through the passage of time, changing in small ways as the generations within the town families came and went, losing the old and bringing in the new. The wheel of the old mill on the river circled endlessly as the current turned it ever onward, the baker's shop stoked fires before dawn that brought villagers in for warm bread, the tailor's sewing machines hummed to life, and the villagers met with one another at the well in the center of Zorion to talk and stay closely connected.

A young girl of about thirteen stood before the water well one fine summer's morning, as the golden rays of a new day spilled over the far-reaching farmlands, filtered through the expanse of leafy trees along the river bank, and found their way around the scattered buildings in the center of the village.

She had long black hair, loosely tied behind her neck, and it hung down her back to her waist. Her skin was fair, and her eyes were as green as the water in the river. She wore a cobalt blue tunic with a red trim. The material reached down almost to her knees, laying over a pair of dark cream colored wide pants, and on her feet were soft black suede cloth boots which laced up her leg underneath. Her form was fit, and she was strong.

The girl was just drawing up a bucket of water when her attention shifted. The chorus of morning birdsong around her had been muffled by the thud of heavy footsteps which sounded behind her, first at a distance, and then coming nearer to her. She turned her head and looked over her shoulder only to find the face of a man who was the only man in the village who could stop her in her tracks.

He was her father's age, weary worn by time and work, with eyes that were bright blue and once-brown hair which was sifted through with streaks of grey and hints of white. His strong frame had taken on the extra weight of age, and his hands were calloused and rough looking. It was none of these things that stopped her, frozen in place for a long moment every time she saw him, but rather one thing which he had not been born with; one thing that had not happened to him naturally over the course of time, and that was a massive scar that ran at an angle down the length of one side of his face from behind his hairline, over his cheek, and down his neck to his collar bone.

It was an old scar and it had faded over the years, but there was still a sort of bruised, purplish and marbled look about it, and it was on his face because of her.

When he saw her, he nodded in greeting. "Padma." His expression did not change. He might have been saying hello to anyone in the village and he treated her no differently than he treated anyone else. That fact was another reason she had such a difficult time facing him.

"Good morning, Omid." She answered him; her heart pounding. With her eyes locked on him, she didn't notice that she hadn't lifter her water bucket up quite as far as she should have to clear it over the edge of the well, and the bottom of the bucket hit the stones on the well's rim, making the water inside slosh around and spill out a bit as she dragged it across.

Without looking away from him, she bent at the waist and set her bucket down on the grass at her feet. He turned his eyes to the well and she blinked and rushed to him, pulling his bucket from his hand.

"Let me get that for you." She insisted as she tugged the pail away from him before he could stop her. Turning her back to him, her breath grew short and her heart raced.

"Padma, you don't have to do that. I can get my own water." He said with a kind, quiet voice as he neared her.

She shook her head adamantly as she hooked the bucket and lowered it down into the well as quickly as she could, cranking the handle on the wheel swiftly. "Oh, it's no trouble. You know I'm glad to help you. I'm always glad to help you."

He breathed a long, almost tired sigh, and she felt her palms grow moist as the bucket grew heavy, and then she hoisted it back up. With her heart nearly working its way out of her chest, she turned and handed the full bucket of water to the big man before her.

"Here you go. No trouble at all." She told him in an easy tone that was edged thickly with tension.

Omid slid his thick fingers under the handle of the bucket and he took it from her, gazing down at her with a sort of sad frown at the corners of his mouth. "Padma…" he began hesitantly, "you don't have to try to do so much for me. You owe me nothing."

She felt her throat tighten and her breath got caught in her chest as she looked upward slowly into his bright eyes. "I owe you everything. I owe you my life." She made herself look at the scar stretching over his face and down his neck. It was a wonder that he had lived; that either of them had lived.

"You owe me nothing." He repeated as he shook his head. He turned from her, walking away with a slow and steady gait as the water in his full bucket spilled over the edges here and there.

She watched him go and felt her eyes sting with hot tears. She tried to swallow the lump in her throat, but it wouldn't go away. Her heart ached as she kept her eyes on him until he was gone.

Padma had been a girl of only nine when it had happened; when everything had changed. She had been wild and carefree, strong and brave, and she used to love to play near the edge of the woods. Her father had told her time and again not to go into the woods, especially alone, and she listened for a little while but then she grew curious about what lay just beyond what she could see and one day she went past the edge and wandered in.

It had taken no time at all before she was lost in all the greatness of the forest; every tree looked indistinguishable from the others, the bushes seemed to surround her on all sides and the daylight faded faster in amongst all the growth. There was no way out that she could find, and she became afraid. Light vanished and darkness filled every space around her, and still she was lost.

That was when it happened. There had been a noise in the brush not far from her. A kind of soft rustling noise, and then in the quiet as she stared around her into the dark with wide eyes, she heard sniffing sounds which were followed by low, deep growls. She had been too terrified to move, but she had managed to scream somehow, and the sound of it brought the call of her name from men moving through the blackness of night with torches held high.

The light of the flames danced through the forest, flickering off of the trees and bushes, creating shadows even darker than the night around her. The voices called out again and again while the noises in the brush around her grew louder, and as the voices neared her, so did the growling.

It seemed to happen in an instant; a flash so swift in her memory that it almost didn't seem real. A wolf, bigger than any of the hunter's kills she had ever seen, launched itself from its hiding place in the foliage near her. He had landed almost at her feet, growling, snapping, and biting at her as she screamed in terror, but almost at the same moment that the wolf attacked, the biggest man in the village tore through the trees and grabbed hold of the wolf by the tail, pulling it back on its padded feet just as it was about to sink it's fangs into Padma. She wailed and wept, huddled down against the ground, and the wolf rounded on the man who swung his torch at the creature, hitting it with the fire.

The wolf attacked the man in a blur of teeth and claws, and the man yelled and fought back against the beast until finally the great wolf fell to the ground in a silent heap and the man pushed himself up from the forest floor.

He came to her then and scooped her up, and she thought she knew who it was until she saw that his face, his head, and his neck were torn open, his lifeblood pouring from him, covering them both. He cried out to the other men who were calling to them, among them Padma's father, who rushed to them only moments later as the big man fell against the arms of the other villagers.

Omid had taken months to recover and when he had finally healed there was a scar from the attack that night; a scar that would always be there, right on his face, every time Padma saw him for the rest of their lives. It was a scar that would not be there had she only listened to her father and obeyed him. Guilt had taken hold in her and its grip promised to never let go.

~ 6 ~

She had taken to doing all that she could for Omid at every opportunity, trying at every chance to repay him somehow, to assuage her guilt, to even the score between them, but it was a debt that could not be repaid, no matter how much she tried, no matter what she did, and his sacrifice ate away at her. It felt even worse to her that he waved off all of her attempts, as if saving her had been nothing, as if there was no debt to be repaid, as if it hadn't been her fault at all that he had nearly been killed too and had the physical devastation to show for it. It seemed to her that the harder she tried to repay him, the more it widened the gap of guilt in her because she could see that her continual efforts meant nothing to him and that he did not want to accept any offering of gratitude or obligation from her, leaving her with a bottomless pit inside her heart, and no way to fill it.

With somber silence, she picked up her bucket of water and walked to the baker's shop, wishing that there was some way to repay the unpayable debt she bore heavy on her heart.

Pushing the door of the shop open, she went inside and saw one of her friends standing at a shelf filled with baskets. He was the baker's son, Carmo. In one hand he held a tray fresh from the oven, laden with piping hot rolls. With a cloth in the other hand, he picked the rolls up one by one and set them into the baskets on the shelf. He looked over his shoulder at her and gave her a smile.

"Good morning, Padma." He nodded pleasantly. Though he was two years younger than her, they were good friends.

"Good morning, Carmo." She tried to give him a genuine smile back, though it didn't quite reach her eyes.

He could be politely described as portly; the baker's son. With soft curves to his rounded face, arms, waist, and legs. Upon the top of his head was a crown of dark brown curls, thick and chunky, somewhat unruly, framing his warm brown eyes. His cheeks were pink as he worked at his tray and baskets, feeling the heat come off of them. He wore loose dark brown trousers and a white linen shirt with a few buttons at the neck. On his feet he wore flour dusted dark shoes, and over the back of his head he wore a small mahogany colored cap.

"Bread today? Two?" He asked, finishing the rolls and taking the tray to the counter.

She nodded. "Yes, please." She gave him a cloth sack with a strap on the top of it, and he put two loaves of freshly baked bread into it, handing it back to her. She dropped a few coins in the small bowl at the edge of the counter and waved at him with her free hand as she turned to the door again.

"Thank you, Carmo. I'll see you around later." She headed out of the shop with her water and her bread, and the door closed softly behind her.

Carmo turned his attention back to the work at hand, but as he was reaching for another tray of baked goods on the cooling rack, his father came from the kitchen in the other room and gave him a serious look.

"You'd better go up and see if your grandmother needs anything." He gave the boy a nod and then turned toward the kitchen once more with a ball of dough in his grip and a coating of flour over his hands and up his arms. His father looked like an older, rounder version of Carmo.

"Yes, father." He answered, and wiping his hands clean, he pulled his apron off and set it on the counter before closing his fingers over a delicate pastry and heading for the old wooden stairs in the corner that led up to their home above the bakery.

His grandmother was in her room which was a simple space set off from a few humble rooms; a sitting area and two other small bedrooms. He knocked at her door and she bade him enter.

A grin formed over his round face as Carmo pushed the door open and saw her laying back in her bed. She was resting against a pile of pillows and she was smiling right back at him. They had the same eyes and they were always glad to see one another.

"Hello Gran Saša!" he beamed at her.

"There's my boy. Light of my life. Come tell me how you are this day!" She said in her soft, thin tones. Her body and voice might be frail and weak, but her spirit was strong and beautiful.

Carmo sat at the side of her bed and took her old weathered hand in one of his, while his other hand was behind his back. "It's been a good morning, Gran. I got all the rolls done and I even got my new pastries out in time before Pa came in and started the bread."

"You did?" She asked brightly, her eyes almost twinkling. "How did they come out?"

Beaming with pride, he brought his other hand around to her and opened his fingers. There in his palm was the delicate little pastry he'd brought up with him. It was finely crafted and dusted with a light sugary powder.

She gasped happily, and he handed it to her. "I saved the best one for you, Gran."

"Well this is absolutely perfect! Just look at that! It's so pretty. I'm as proud as popping, my boy." She touched his cheek gently and then lifted the pastry to her mouth, tasting it. Closing her eyes, she tipped her head to one side a little and then to the other.

He watched her with rapt attention, waiting to see what she thought. It had been her bakery many years before and his father had been the boy growing up in it, now he was the boy and his father was the baker.

"It's perfection!" She sighed blissfully as she finished it off. "I love the buttery soft center. What a great invention!" She waved him to her and he leaned close and hugged her carefully.

"I used your old recipe and just made a few little changes to it." He admitted with a grin.

"Well it's your new recipe now and I think you should make lots of them and keep them on the shelf because the whole village will be wanting to eat them all up in no time!" She laughed lightly and reached to hold his hand again.

"I'll do that, Gran. Thank you." He felt as if he had just won the whole world. "How are you feeling today?"

She shrugged a little and looked away from him. "Oh, probably better than I'll feel tomorrow, but much better now that I've had a treat from you!"

Concern crossed his brow and he studied her closely. "Do you need anything?" He asked, holding her hand just a little tighter in his.

Gran shook her head slightly. "Just rest. There's not much else to do at this point, I'm afraid. What's best for me now is rest and good company, especially when my good company brings me things like you did!"

Carmo smiled and nodded but the worry and fear in his heart grew, as it did every day when he looked closely at her. The doctor had told them that she wouldn't be with them much longer and there was nothing Carmo wished for more than to have her stay with him as long as he could keep her in the world.

They talked a while about little things and then his father called him from downstairs. His grandmother gave him a big smile.

"You'd better go help him. You know he needs you." She winked at Carmo.

"But you need me too!" Carmo pleaded quietly.

Gran shook her head. "I'll rest. You can come to see me later. Now kiss me and off you go."

Carmo kissed her cheek and gave her a smile before hurrying down the stairs to see what his father wanted. There was a basket waiting for him on the edge of the counter.

"Take that over to the tailor's shop please." His father called out from the kitchen.

"Yes, father!" Carmo answered back loudly, scooping the basket onto his arm and going to the door.

The tailor's shop was a short way down the small road, just a few buildings past the bakery. Zorion was built a little differently than most villages, which have a condensed town center. All of the shops and buildings in the center of the village where most commerce took place were all spaced a bit apart from each other, with a small grassy mound between shops here, and a pretty garden tucked in between some buildings there, so that there was a little bit of a walk between them, just beneath a few shady trees now and then.

Carmo entered the tailor's shop and looked around. There were a few well-crafted articles of clothing hanging on display throughout the room; a fine coat in one place, a pair of good trousers in another, and some dresses with full skirts and curling ruffles.

At one of the far corners of the room stood a great mirror where a visitor to the tailor's shop might see a reflection of themselves with a certain kind of material or some premade clothing.

Standing before the mirror was a tall, thin boy with dark brown hair which was combed back from his hairline and cut short at the collar. His thin lips were pursed thoughtfully as his blue eyes studied his reflection meticulously. Held up against his body was a swath of dark green brushed silk.

"Good morning Evren!" Carmo piped up, going to him and standing behind him. Carmo met Evren's light gaze in the mirror. Evren furrowed his brow.

"The Lord Mayor special ordered this silk and it took ages to come in. He wants it for a new waistcoat. It's more money than I make in a month here, but I just love it. Look at this," he widened his eyes and brought the material up close to his face, "does it bring my eyes out? It does, doesn't it? I was wondering if they had any in blue silk, because I think that would look even better on me, but I do love the green so much. I wish I had both of them. All of them, actually... there is a whole shelf of special materials in the back that are rare and beautiful, and I want them all. Every single one of them would make me look so much better." He pouted slightly as he regarded himself critically. "The clothes make the man, you know."

Carmo tilted his head slightly and gave Evren a curious look. "I think you look just fine in what you're wearing. That's very nice." He nodded to the trousers and well-made shirt that Evren had on underneath the cloth which was draped over him.

Evren sighed heavily and narrowed his eyes. "Well it's fine for working in here, and it is nice; I made sure the tailor used the best material that I could afford, but it's not nearly as nice as I want it to be. Just imagine how beautiful I could be if I was able to dress in what I want. It's not just the clothing that needs to be better; I want a bigger body, not this skinny rail of a frame that I have. You know, strong muscles and good form, and the finest clothes that money can buy. I'd be at my best then, wouldn't I?" He mused wishfully as he gazed at his reflection.

Carmo remained puzzled. "I think you're just fine like you are, but I don't know that much about dressing nice."

The taller boy turned then and faced the younger boy. Evren, like Padma, was two years older than Carmo. "What we look like on the outside tells others a lot about who we are. It creates a first impression. I want everyone to think well of me when they see me. I want everyone to respect me. If I want that, I have to dress nice and show them what I'm worth."

Biting his lower lip a bit, Carmo considered what Evren said, wondering about it. He let his thoughts and questions about it go and he blinked, remembering that he had come with bread for Evren and his master, the tailor.

"I've brought your bread." He smiled, holding out the sack he had in his hand.

Evren nodded and took it from him, giving him a few coins for it. "Good, thank you. The master will be wanting his breakfast soon, and some for lunch as well no doubt."

Setting the bread on the counter, he went back to the material, wrapping himself in it and looking back at the mirror. "Isn't it beautiful?" He asked wistfully.

"It is. I hope you can get the things you want." Carmo smiled at him. "I better go back to the bakery. I guess we'll see you later?" He asked. Evren nodded absentmindedly.

"Yes, I'll see you later." The taller boy said to his reflection in the mirror, though the comment was directed at his younger friend.

Carmo smiled to himself and walked out of the shop, but just as he was about to close the door, another of his friends was walking up the path to the door, so he held the door for her.

"Good morning, Carmo!" She smiled sweetly at him.

"Good morning, Hanne!" Carmo replied, giving her a lighthearted smile.

Hanne wore a simple dress, slightly faded, set about with printed flowers on the material. Her brown hair was parted down the middle and plaited, hanging over the front of her shoulders to her waist.

She stepped in through the door and faced Carmo as she did so. "Where are you off to?" She asked curiously.

"Oh, well I came to bring some bread, but I've done that, so now I've got to get back to the bakery." He shrugged with an easy smile.

"We'll see you later won't we?" Hanne raised her brows expectantly. Carmo nodded.

"Yes!" He waved as he headed down the steps toward the road.

Hanne closed the door of the tailor's shop and looked over at Evren, who was petting the material in his hands lovingly. "I should be dressed head to toe in this." He sighed as he put the material back up on the shelf and walked over to the counter.

Hanne admired the brushed green silk with an appreciative look and then turned toward him. "It is lovely material. Are you going to make some clothes out of it?" She gave him a hopeful smile.

"Not until I make ten times the money I'm making now. Someday I'm going to be so wealthy that I will be able to buy everything I want and then I'll be completely happy." For a passing moment Evren let himself daydream about what it would be like and then he came back to the business at hand and turned his attention to Hanne.

"What brings you in today?" He asked, glancing for a fraction of a second at her dress. It was worn, but it was clean and pressed. He knew that her family didn't have the money to buy new material often. They had several children and the clothes were often passed down from one to the next, though as Hanne was the oldest of them, she was most often in the newer material when they had the means to get it.

Lowering her hand to smooth it over her frock, she spoke with a soft voice. "I was thinking that maybe I could talk with you about getting a new dress. I've saved up some extra money and I was hoping that it would be enough to get something really nice made."

Evren was surprised but pleased to hear it. "A day dress? Something like this, simple and easy that you could work in?"

Raising her brown eyes to meet his light gaze, she shook her head slowly. "No, not really. I mean, I know it's terribly impractical, but I was thinking that maybe it could be something a little nicer."

Tipping his head interestedly, he eyed her closely. "Something for special events?"

Hanne shook her head again. "Maybe… something really nice. Something flattering. Something very… pretty." Her heart began to pound as her cheeks blushed a soft rosy shade.

Evren nodded slowly then as he realized what she was talking about. "Something to turn someone's head?" He asked with a confidential quietness to his voice.

She pressed her lips together into a thin line. "Perhaps…" She trailed off quietly.

"Something to turn Sevahn's head?" He asked hesitantly.

Hanne looked down at her hands, held together in front of her for a moment before she returned her gaze to Evren and answered him. "He doesn't notice me now. He only has eyes for Padma. She doesn't want him. She doesn't care about him at all. He doesn't seem to notice that though. I like him so much." She frowned and her shoulders slumped downward. "I just thought… if I was in a pretty dress, if I looked… nicer. Then maybe he might…" She trailed off again.

Evren finished her sentence for her. "Then he might notice you and like you."

She nodded. "I just wish so much that he loved me too. I think he could, if he only gave it half a chance."

Evren lifted his chin. "Well I understand that. I'll see what I can find for you. I promise you that I will do my best to help you."

With a grateful smile, she nodded at him. "Thank you. I know it's terribly impractical of me, but I've just got to do something."

Before Evren could reply, there was a soft scraping sound and they both turned toward the front of the store. A small face poked through the opening at the door and brown eyes exactly the same as Hanne's were locked on her.

"Petia!" She gasped disapprovingly at her little sister. "I told you to wait outside until I was done."

The little girl nodded. "I know, and I was waiting for you like you said, but Sevahn is coming down the road!" Hanne's younger sister looked quite excited about it. Petia was eight years old and she didn't think there was anyone in the whole world as wonderful as her sister Hanne, so she followed her everywhere. Hanne tolerated it to an extent, but time on her own was precious to her as a result.

Hanne's face grew pale and her breath grew short. "He's out there? He's coming?"

Petia nodded excitedly and waved her small hand, beckoning her sister out of the tailor's shop. Hanne turned to look at Evren apologetically. "Sorry, I'll catch up with you later."

He shrugged and smiled. "I'll be there."

Hanne rushed out of the shop and Petia stayed fifteen paces behind her as her sister insisted that she do. The older girl hurried after a tall, muscular, well built boy with wavy golden hair. He was walking after Padma, who was heading toward her home, having finished her chores in the village for the morning.

"Padma!" He called out to her, picking up his pace to catch up to her.

"Sevahn!" Hanne called after him.

Padma stopped and looking over her shoulder and saw him coming after her. She sighed and looked away, but she stayed where she was and waited for him. He caught up to her, breathless and smiling wide.

"Padma!" He gushed, his eyes moving over her face as if he was trying to memorize everything about her.

"Sevahn!" Hanne called out, just catching up with him and Padma. Padma smiled widely at her and reached her arms out to hug her friend.

"Hanne! Good morning!" She grinned pleasantly. Then she looked over at Sevahn, whose gaze was locked on her. "Hello Sevahn."

Petia stopped fifteen paces behind the small group and watched them, her eyes wide and her hands clasped in front of her.

"What did you need?" Padma asked Sevahn. He caught his breath and tried to look casual as he glanced uncertainly at Hanne and then turned more toward Padma.

"I was hoping that you could meet up with me later. Out by the old stables." He gave her a lopsided smile and it was clear that he was accustomed to that smile of his having an immediate effect on any girl he flashed it for. It had no effect on Padma, but Hanna looked as if she had lost her breath.

Padma shook her head. "Sorry, I have a lot to do. I don't have time to go out there with you." She looked at Hanne and gave her a nod. "See you." She turned then and left them and Sevahn sighed wistfully.

He trudged slowly to the water well and Hanne followed close behind him, trying to match his steps to be at his side. "I'm not too busy today!" She told him with a hopeful smile. "I... I could meet you out at the old stables! Then... then you wouldn't be out there alone." Her cheeks turned a light pink and she grinned up at him.

Sevahn barely glanced at her. Instead, he looked hard at the bucket in his hand and concentrated on lowering it

~ 18 ~

into the well. "No. You should stay in the village and take care of your sister." He grumbled.

Hanne felt her stomach tighten with nerves as embarrassment washed over her. She watched in silence as Sevahn took his water bucket and walked back toward his home. Petia came up beside her and took her hand, giving it a little squeeze. "You really are too good for him. He doesn't deserve you."

Just then another boy came to the well. He was a little tall for twelve years old, with strong muscles though he was lean, and longer dark brown hair that hung about his head in gentle locks, reaching his eyes, the middle of his ears, and the bottom of his neck. He had warm brown eyes and a kind smile. His skin was dark golden brown, partly due to his heritage and partly due to the fact that he spent so much time outside in the sun.

"I'll have to agree with your sister about that." He spoke with a friendly tone. "You deserve better than him."

Hanne turned with a start and looked at him. "Amias!" A smile formed over her face. He gave her a nod as he filled his water bucket.

"Good morning Hanne, good morning Petia." He greeted them both. Petia beamed at him and Hanne looked him over lightly.

"You've already been out to all of your traps?" She asked in surprise. "It's so early!"

He nodded and indicated the two dead rabbits he had tied on a thin rope that hung over his shoulder. On a similar strand of rope tied around his waist, he held up a length of it that was heavy with five good sized fish. "I've done well in the traps and I caught these this morning. It's been a good day and it's just gotten started. Why don't you take the rabbits to your mother? I won't eat all of this today and I still have other traps to check further down the river in a bit."

Amias handed her the rope that had the two rabbits tied to it and she took it with a grateful smile. "Thank you. I know she can make a good stew out of them for dinner tonight."

Amias shrugged lightly. "I'm glad someone will get some use out of them."

Petia tugged at Hanne's arm. "Come on, let's go take the rabbits home and then play! I've been waiting all morning!"

Hanne nodded and laughed. "Okay, okay. We can go." She looked over at Amias as she turned to leave with her little sister. "Thank you for the rabbits. We'll see you back here in a while?" She asked curiously.

"I'll be here." He nodded and waved to her, filling his water bucket and then turning to leave. He was a good-looking boy with fine features and he had a gentle soul. He was wiser than his years, patient with those around him, and cleverer than any other young one in the village. Amias was a friend to all and they were all friends of his in return.

He left the well with his pail of water and his fish dangling from the rope around his waist. He carried a sack over one shoulder; it was filled with traps and various things that he used whenever he went out into the woods or along the river. He had been a hunter and fisher since he was a young boy and he'd gotten better at it with every year.

Amias waved to people that he passed here and there, and he walked along through the village until he came to the far end of the long road, near the river, to a humble home. It had once been a barn; two stories tall, but part of it had been converted into a home for himself and his uncle to live in. They still kept one cow in the other side of the barn, closed off from the home, and she provided milk for them.

He reached his hand for the latch on the door and pressed his lips together into a tight line as he opened the door quietly. With silent footsteps he entered the home, closing the door behind him.

It was dark inside though shafts of sunlight peeked through cracks in the wood here and there. He looked around and then carefully placed his feet one after the other on the quietest spots on the floor, so as not to disturb his uncle.

The older man was passed out on a bench near the table, with an empty bottle in his hand. He was snoring loudly and from the smell of the bottle and the man, Amias knew that his uncle hadn't gone to bed, he'd stayed up all night into the morning, drinking until he passed out.

Amias knew that he should have used his own secret entrance into the house; the one that went straight into his room. He'd used it to leave that morning, not wanting to wake his uncle so early before dawn, but he hadn't realized that his uncle would still be passed out.

He headed for the kitchen and put the fish in a container of water, setting the bucket from the well on the table. With a sigh, he went to his room and closed the door behind him.

Taking an apple from his pocket, he bit into it and opened the secret door to his room; the one leading outside. He let the warm sunshine spill in and he leaned his head against the frame of the little door and thought about his parents. He barely remembered them being together, he had been so little when they had all been a family, but then everything changed.

His mother had grown very sick one winter and she hadn't had the strength to make it through to spring. She passed away while the snow was still blowing, and it had been too hard on his father. His father left to go find his fortune wherever he could, and he said he would come back someday.

Every day when Amias woke, he looked up at the sun as it rose over the farmlands to the east and he whispered to himself, "Maybe today... maybe he will come back today." Every day he wished it and every night he told himself that the next day might make his wish come true.

Chapter Two

The Stranger's Tale

The day burned away quickly as all the friends did their chores and one by one reached the late afternoon when they were free to do as they liked. They all met up at the water well in the center of town, as they often did, so that they could spend time together.

Hanne was braiding Padma's long dark hair as Carmo and Petia played cat's cradle with a length of string. Amias whittled away at a piece of wood, carving it into an arrow for his bow. They chatted idly amongst themselves as they waited for Evren, who came strolling down the lane to them with a smile and a wave of his hand.

When Evren reached them, everyone looked up at him and Carmo brightened and grinned with enthusiasm.

"I was waiting until we were all here before I told any of you. I heard father talking to Anna, the innkeeper from the inn, this afternoon. She was telling him about the stranger that arrived today. They get travelers at the inn all the time, but she said this one was different. She said she'd never seen anyone like him before. She thinks he's some kind of warrior or knight." Carmo's eyes were alight with admiration.

All of the friends perked up at the story he shared with them, all of them staring at him with curiosity.

"Have you seen him?" Petia asked, leaning closer to him.

"What does he look like?" Evren intoned interestedly.

"Where is he from?" Hanne chimed in with an eager smile.

Carmo only shrugged and shook his head. "I don't know. I only heard them talking about him for a moment."

Padma's mouth curled up at the sides and she eyed the rest of them with excitement. "We know he's at the inn, so let's go have a look! Maybe we'll see him!"

The idea took no further encouragement. All of the friends stood up and hurried together toward the inn at the south edge of the village. They rarely went there as it wasn't in a direction any of them would normally go during their day, and their favorite spots to spend time with one another were at the east side of the village nearer the river.

When they arrived at the inn, they all slowed their running to a walking pace and Petia worked to catch up with them. Their eyes were all turned toward the big old wooden structure with rooms for travelers on the second floor and a dining hall and pub on the first floor. Off to the right side of the main building was a stable for horses and carriages, and to the left of the building, opening from wide sliding doors from the dining hall and pub, was a garden with wooden tables and benches.

There didn't seem to be anyone around that they could see, and they stopped short outside of the inn, looking up at it hesitantly.

"Do you suppose he's in there?" Hanne asked quietly, gazing at the windows of the rooms above the dining hall and not seeing any with candlelight glowing from them.

"Well he must be," Padma stated flatly, placing her hands on her hips, "so let's go ask." She marched into the front door of the inn then, and the others stared after her in surprise and then followed along behind her with Amias taking up the last behind Petia.

They stopped at the bar where the innkeeper, Anna, was pouring a tall glass of beer. She looked down at them and gave them a friendly nod. "Hello you lot. What are you doing about here this afternoon?"

The friends exchanged uncertain glances with one another and Evren lifted his chin and spoke with shallow confidence. "Hello Anna. We were wondering if we could sit and have some tea here."

Though every one of the friends was surprised, none of them looked it and all of them kept their watch on Anna, who was more than a little bemused.

"You want tea?" She asked, humoring them. None of them had ever set so much as a foot in the inn before, unless they were running a quick errand for one of the adults in the village.

"Yes, please." Padma jumped in, looking and sounding every bit as if she meant it.

Anna's brows furrowed as she considered the request and then she sighed and nodded. "All right. Fine. Would you like tea inside here in the dining room or outside by the fire?"

It was then that Petia tugged hard at Hanne's sleeve and Hanne tried to ignore her as she paid attention to what was going on before her, but Petia only tugged harder and then finally nudged her sister's foot.

Hanne turned sharply toward her younger sister with an exasperated look. "What is it?"

~ 25 ~

Petia subtly jerked her head toward the fire pit outside in the garden and Hanne looked up, her mouth falling open in surprise. There by the fire pit was a big man; the biggest she had ever seen, wearing a dark black coat and a wide brimmed black hat that was tugged low over his face. She could see that he had darker skin and black hair that was long and hung down his back and the sides of his obscured face, almost to his elbows.

"Inside, thank you." Evren replied to Anna.

"Outside, please." Hanne answered swiftly, speaking over the last of Evren's words. He turned to her with a questioning look only to see over her shoulder what it was that had captured her attention.

Anna frowned at them. "Well which is it? Inside or outside?"

"Outside." They all answered, having looked over and seen the stranger at the fire pit.

Anna followed their gaze and sighed, crossing her arms over her chest. "Now, I've got a guest out there. Don't you lot go bothering him and needling him with questions. You have your tea on your own, do you hear me?" Her voice was menacing.

Every one of them turned their faces back to her. "Yes missus." They answered her.

She rolled her eyes and shook her head as she walked toward the stove and the kettle. "Off you go then. Go and sit at a table there and don't bother him."

Padma and Evren walked out of the dining hall first, through the wide-open doors and into the garden, and the others followed them. Together they sat at a table near the stranger, all of them sneaking glances at him while trying not to stare. He did not look up at them.

"It was clever of you to say we were here for tea." Hanne gave Evren a smile.

He shrugged as if it was nothing while simultaneously looking quite pleased with himself. "I had to think of something. I don't think Anna would have let us in otherwise. It was quite clever of me if I do say so myself."

They all looked over their shoulders at the stranger who continued to hold his mug of beer in his hand and contemplate it without raising his head.

"He's very big, don't you think?" Evren said, peering at the stranger closely. "He's not heavy... but he's big. Like a soldier."

"Like a warrior." Carmo added, looking from the stranger back to Evren.

"I wish I looked like that." Evren sighed plaintively.

The stranger raised his head slowly then, looking up at them with a pair of piercing dark eyes. They were warm and mysterious. The man's face was strong and solid, as if he had been chiseled out of dark marble. His eyes met Evren's and he shared a look with him until Evren look away, breathless and trembling.

"Here's your tea." Anna said, and all the friends jumped, for they had been so wrapped up in the stranger that they had not even noticed her coming with a tray for them.

She set their cups around them and they shared glances with each other. She poured their tea for them and then set the teapot in the center of the table along with some toast and biscuits.

"Innkeeper." A deep voice sounded, and all the children looked up to see the stranger standing beside their table. "Please put their refreshment on my bill."

Anna looked up at the stranger who towered over her, seeming to fill all of the sky behind him. She nodded. "Yes, I'll do that. Shall I send them inside? Would you prefer privacy?"

He gave his head a shake. "I'd prefer to join them, if I may." He turned his dark eyes from her to them, looking briefly at each of them.

His gaze was fathoms deep and there was something peculiar about it, but there was a welcoming kindness in his smile.

The friends all gave each other a quick look and nodded to one another, moving aside so that there was room for him to sit between Hanne and Carmo, who was dwarfed by the great man.

The stranger set his mug of ale on the table before him and all their eyes locked on him. Anna only gave them a puzzled frown before turning and walking away.

"Thank you for letting me join you. I'm glad for your company." He reached up and pushed his wide brimmed black hat backward some, revealing most of his face. He was strikingly handsome in a noble way, but there was something about him that seemed different than anyone they had ever seen before.

"I am Nassim." He told them, looking from each of them to the next.

"I'm Hanne, and this is my sister Petia." Hanne replied in a soft voice, gazing up at the man near her. "This is Padma and Evren, that's Amias, and that's Carmo." She introduced them all and they didn't bother to hide the fascination on their faces.

"Where are you from?" Evren asked, folding his hands around his teacup and speaking with a near breathless tone.

Nassim's voice remained level. "I come from very far away. Farther than you can see on a clear day."

"Where are you going?" Petia asked, her fingers on her lower lip as she gave him a shy smile.

He smiled back at her and leaned his forearms on the table. "I'm going a long way, far up into the Kamala mountains." He narrowed his eyes a little as if he was peering to see as far as he could. "You see that peak?" He pointed to one mountain peak that was higher than the rest near it, looming up behind them far into the reaches of the sky.

All of the children turned and raised their eyes to the mountains behind them. "Yes?" Petia asked curiously. "Is that where you're going?"

"It is. It's quite a long way to go." He answered, reaching for his ale and taking a long drink of it.

"Why are you going up there?" Carmo asked in puzzlement. "I don't think there's anything up there."

A smile spread over Nassim's face and he lowered his eyes from the mountain peak back down to the gazes of the children around him. "Oh, there's something up there; something very special."

"What is it?" Padma asked, watching him in fascination.

He waved his hand in the air dismissively. "Oh, nothing that would interest any of you. You have good lives here. You have no need of anything outside of your pretty lives and your village. It would be nothing at all to you."

Evren's brow furrowed. "I have interests outside of the village. Please, Sir. Tell us what it is!" His curiosity, like that of his friends, was piqued. Amias simply sat still, listening and watching. He had not said a word, and he continued to do no more than listen.

Nassim leaned closer to them, closing the circle of their heads as if he were imparting a great secret to them. "Well, if you are so interested to know then I shall tell you, but you must not tell anyone else."

"Oh, we swear! We wouldn't!" Hanne promised with wide, serious eyes.

The afternoon light had faded by then and the sky began to grow darker as the stars came out. The flames near them in the firepit crackled and sparked, glowing bright orange and casting strange shadows around them in the fading light.

The man spoke in his deep, low tone. "I am going there to find the Wish Weaver."

All of the children stared at him in silence for a moment, but then finally Padma spoke. "Who is the Wish Weaver?"

The stranger looked mildly surprised. "Have you never heard of her?"

Five faces around him shook an answer of no, and Amias stayed still and watched the man. "No, we haven't." Petia answered for them.

Nassim nodded slowly. "Then I shall tell you. The Wish Weaver is an old woman who lives up at the peak on the other side of Stargazer Lake. She is special… she has magic. People who go to see her ask her to weave their wishes and dreams into reality, and she does. I am going to seek her out so that she will weave my wishes into reality. I want very much for them to come true."

"A woman who weaves wishes into being?" Padma asked in breathless wonder. "At what cost?"

"At no cost. It is what she does." Nassim reassured her. "But it's a very long way to go. It's dangerous."

"But you get whatever you wish for, no matter what it is?" Evren asked anxiously, his eyes big with wonder and hope.

"If you get to her, yes." Nassim nodded, tipping his ale back and swallowing much of it. "There's a trail that starts off up the Kamalas and it's just outside of this village, across the ford on the mountain river. From there it's quite a journey straight up the mountain to the very top."

He stood up then and set his tankard down heavily on the thick wood. "I wouldn't recommend anyone going who didn't have tremendous courage and experience in the forest. They might not make it back, but if they did…" He trailed off eyeing all of them seriously, "their wishes would be woven into being."

Nassim walked toward the wide-open door then, heading back into the inn, but he turned and looked over his shoulder once at them, his dark eyes shining as brightly as the stars above. "I wish you well, all of you." His tone was earnest. Then he rounded a corner and disappeared, leaving them at their table with their tea.

There was silence around the table for a long moment as the group of friends looked around at one another.

"We should go." Evren said quietly, with shallow breath and a pounding heart.

"We have no business going." Amias stated flatly as he reached for his tea. "We do not know if the traveler is telling us the truth, and even if there is a Wish Weaver up at the top of the mountain, no one does anything without cost."

"But we could have our wishes granted to us if she's there!" Padma's voice was strong. "Imagine... if it's true... if we could go up there and find her, if we could have any wish we wanted come true!" She shook her head and stared at the peak far up behind the village. "Just... imagine."

"I could wish my Gran well." Carmo whispered as he too stared up at the lofty peak.

"I could wish to be wealthy and beautiful; strong like Nassim." Evren spoke as if he were in a trance just thinking about it.

"What would you wish for?" Petia turned to Hanne and asked, though she looked as if she already knew the answer.

Hanne sighed and her shoulders slumped slightly. "I would wish for someone special to love me."

Hanne looked at Padma. "What about you? What would you wish for?"

Padma's face darkened as she looked down at the table. "I would wish for the past to be different."

Evren turned to Amias. "Amias, what would you wish for?"

Amias shook his head. "There is nothing I would wish for. All of our successes, all of our happiness, all of that comes into being because we make it so. It doesn't matter if there's an old woman weaving wishes into reality at the top of the mountain peak or not; no one does anything without a price. We should earn what we desire and if it does not come to us then it is not meant for us."

His friends stared at him. Padma frowned at him. "There's nothing that you would wish for? Given anything your heart desires?"

Amias considered it for a moment and let out a sigh. "If I was being selfish I would wish for my father to return, but I don't want him to come back unless it's his choice, not my wish. I would only want him here if he was here by his own accord, because it was what he wanted, not because it's what I would want."

Carmo gave him a heartfelt smile. "I understand. I hope he comes back soon too."

Evren straightened his shoulders. "Well, I think it would be worth the journey. I have wishes and I would want them to come true if there was any way to make that happen. Now we know there's a way. I think we should go. I think that we should all go together." He looked around the table at the others who stared back at him in wonder.

"It's so far, do you think we could make it?" Hanne asked hesitantly.

"We'd be together. It's much closer to us than it is to Nassim; he came much further than we would go. I think we should do it." Evren was sounding even more sure of his proposition.

"I want to go." Padma agreed firmly as she pressed her lips into a thin line.

"Me too." Hanne added, looking at Padma and then Evren.

Petia gasped in horror. "We can't go all the way up there! Mama would never let us!"

"You wouldn't be going, Petia. You'd have to stay here in the village. It's much too dangerous." Hanne cast a sympathetic but unwavering look to her sister.

"It's much too dangerous for all of you. You shouldn't go." Amias told them in a warning tone. "I know it sounds like an easy fix and a wonderful thing, but go home and sleep on it. Sense will come to you in the morning."

The others didn't say anything, they only finished their tea as each of them focused their thoughts on what it would be like to have their wishes granted freely to them. The group left the inn and bid each other a good night as they all went to their homes, their minds so wrapped up in wishes that the ideas invaded their dreams. All but Amias. He went home and looked up at the stars, knowing that his father was somewhere beneath them, and hoping that someday they would see each other again.

Chapter Three

A Wishful Journey Begins

Morning light shone through the small bedroom, illuminating the old worn quilt that covered the bed and the old woman in it. The door creaked open quietly and soft footsteps sounded, followed by a hushed voice.

"Gran... Gran!" Carmo reached his hand out to Saša and she opened her eyes and smiled up at him.

"Good morning my darling boy!" She blinked a few times and did her best to push herself up on her pillows so that she could look at him properly. When she did, her smile faded.

"What's on your mind young one?" She asked with a note of foreboding in her voice.

Carmo stammered a little and drew in a shaky breath as he stepped toward her. "There was a stranger at the inn last night. A traveling man. We all talked with him. He said that he was on his way to the highest peak in the Kamala's. He said there's an old woman there that he's going to see. A Wish Weaver. She weaves wishes into reality. Have you ever heard of her?"

Saša frowned and sat up as straight as she could. "No, I haven't, but there's a great deal in this world that I don't know about." Her brow furrowed. "What do you think of his story?"

Carmo didn't speak for a moment. He was trying to find the courage and the words to tell her what was in his heart. "I... believe him. My friends and I..." he hesitated, taking a deep breath, "well, we were thinking of going to see her ourselves."

The old woman shook her head and reached for the boy's hand. "You shouldn't go. You should stay here at home where you belong. There's nothing for you out there, Carmo."

Disappointment drew his expression downward. "But they're going to go. It would be safer if we all went together. We'd just go straight to her and get our wishes and come back."

Saša eyed him thoughtfully. "And why would you go? What is it that you would risk so much to wish for?"

"I would wish you well. I would wish that you could live a long while." He answered quietly.

A small smile came over her face and she reached both arms out to him and drew him close to her in a warm embrace. "Dear boy. You are such a dear boy." Running her hand over the back of his head, she spoke in a gentle voice. "I don't have much time left in this world. My wish would be that I could spend all of the time that I have left with you, and that's a wish that could come true."

He leaned up and looked desperately at her. "But if I go and get my wish, then we'll have lots of time together and you'll be well again! It wouldn't have to only be a short while! I would make the journey for that wish to come true, to have you longer. I would go! I want to go. I want to try!"

He meant it. He meant every word of it and she could hear it in his voice. She shook her head as a tear formed in her eye.

"Please don't go, my dear boy. Please stay here with me and let's spend the last of our time together." She squeezed his hands gently with hers, begging him to stay.

Carmo hesitated, searching her old eyes and her withered face. His mind was tumbling with possibility. "Gran, I want you here with me for a long time and no matter what I have to sacrifice to make that happen, I'm willing to do it. I don't care about the journey and I know I would be safe with my friends, but the most important thing is keeping you here with me, healthy and strong, for years to come. I can wish for that. The Wish Weaver can make that wish come true."

She hugged him tight to her heart. "Don't go, my Carmo. Please don't go."

Amias stepped from his bedroom in the barn house and looked around the kitchen. Nothing had changed since the day before. No food had been touched and the only water gone from the pail he had taken to the well was the water that he had used himself. His uncle was not at home. He wondered briefly if he was working or out somewhere with a bottle in his hand, but the thought left him as he went to the other side of the barn where the cow and chickens were, to collect eggs and milk for his breakfast.

When he was fed, he picked up the water pail and gave the remainder of the water to the animals and then walked into the village to refill the pail. He was surprised when he got to the well, to see all of his friends there together.

"What are you all doing here?" He asked as his stomach tightened with realization. He already knew the answer and he almost didn't want to hear them say it.

Hanne looked up at him. "We're planning the trip. We're going to go, Amias."

Padma gave him a hopeful smile. "Come with us, won't you please? You can't stay behind here while we go. We do everything together."

Evren nodded. "We need you, Amias. You know we do. Come with us!"

Amias lowered his pail into the well and it splashed as it hit the water's surface. "I'm not going, and neither should any of you."

"We're going." Evren replied evenly. "With or without you, but we do wish that it was with you."

Carmo spoke up then. "The traveler Nassim is gone. He left this morning. If we go, we go on our own. We couldn't catch up to him now to travel with him."

Padma lifted her chin and spoke confidently. "We can make it on our own if we go together. We can do this."

"You shouldn't do this." Amias said without looking at any of them as he hoisted his bucket up out of the well.

"We're doing it." Padma answered him.

"We'll leave tonight, if you are all in agreement." Evren told them quietly. "After our families are all in bed. We'll meet up at the edge of the wood and sleep there until dawn, and then make our way."

"I'm going." Each one of them answered, looking around at the others. All except Amias.

He sighed heavily and gave them all a disappointed look. "Be safe. There's much more out there in the woods and on the mountain than you know."

~ 38 ~

With that he turned and walked back to his home at the barn to leave the pail of water before going to check all his traps and go fishing.

The day burned away and Amias made a point of not going to see any of his friends in their daily routines; knowing where they would be and when. He left them all to themselves as his mind and heart wrestled with the knowledge he had of their plan.

When darkness came he sat at the secret door in his room and looked up at the night sky, for the first time not thinking of his father but rather of his friends who were going to be leaving in mere hours for the highest peak in the Kamala mountains. He knew that they would be in over their heads. Of all of them, he was the one with the most experience in the forest and on the river. He knew more of the dangers nearby the village in the forest; dangers that they could face, and he was certain that there must be far greater risk beyond the safer boundaries of the area where they lived.

He tried not to think of any of it; where they would go and what could happen to them. He tried to tell himself that they would become afraid and turn back to the village and that it would be all right again. Even though he tried to console himself with these thoughts, his heart stiffened in fear at the knowledge of what could come.

* * *

Hanne slipped her bag over her torso and tied her soft leather boots tight around her calves. She was feeling a mixture of excitement, fear, anxiety, and uncertainty, but she knew that if she could make it to the Wish Weaver, her hopes of being loved by Sevahn would come to pass, and she wanted nothing so much as that.

Listening carefully to be sure that everyone else in her house was asleep, she padded softly to the back door where she knew she could get away unseen and unheard.

Just as she opened the door to leave, she felt a familiar tug on her dress and she turned sharply to see her sister looking up at her with big, tearful eyes. On her shoulder she had a small sack which was rounded at the bottom with some of her belongings.

Her heart twisted in her chest. "Petia, you can't come. You have to stay here. It's not safe for you, and Mama will need help with the others. Please just stay here, be safe, and I'll be home soon. Quicker than you can imagine."

"No!" Petia insisted in a loud whisper. "I'm coming with you! Don't make me stay here by myself! I want to go too!"

Hanne sighed and wrapped her arms around her younger sister, giving her a big hug. When she let her go, she held the girls' face in her hands. "You're not coming. That's all there is to it. Now go on and go back upstairs. When I come back I'll bring something for you from the journey."

"I don't want anything except to be with you!" Petia insisted.

Hanne shook her head and spoke firmly. "No. You're staying here and that's all there is to it. Don't tell anyone where I've gone. I'll be back soon. Be good. I love you."

With that she gave her sister a little push back into the house and closed the door between them, feeling an ache in her heart as she did. It was sharpened by the sound of

Petia's miserable weeping and her small face at the window, watching as Hanne left.

When Hanne reached the well she found the others there waiting for her; Padma, Evren, and Carmo. They looked upon one another with determination in their eyes and together they set out under the cover of darkness with only moonlight to brighten the path before them.

Though the night was filled with the call of owls and notes of crickets, the wind rustling through leaves and the constant rush of the river, the friends made no sounds other than their footsteps, not wanting to attract any attention to themselves. Even their breathing was shallow and soft, their breath almost held as they left the familiarity of their small village and ventured further toward a world they knew nothing of.

With the village recessed at their backs, they entered the edge of the great forest where the trees grew sparse and the bushes were big and full. They walked in single file together until the moonlight began to grow dim through the thickening woods, and there Hanne finally spoke.

"I think that we should stop here for the night. It's getting hard to see and I'm not sure I want to travel so far in the dark." Her voice, though quiet, seemed to echo off the trees and sounded much louder than she meant for it to.

Evren and Padma turned to her and dropped their bags to the ground. "I agree, I think we should stay here for the night." Padma replied, looking around pensively at the darkness enveloping them and remembering with a chill the night when she had been attacked by the wolf.

Carmo sighed with relief and gave his friends a small smile. "I'm glad we're stopping. I'd rather go on in the daylight, if it's all the same to any of you."

Evren shrugged. "We need to rest anyway, if we're going to be up and traveling all day tomorrow."

They arranged their humble campsite as Padma built a small fire for them, and they laid out their blankets on the ground around it.

Hanne looked at her three friends and held up her small sack that she'd brought with her. "I have some food if anyone's hungry. It's not much, but I'm glad to share it. I have some dried meat, nuts, and some apples from our tree."

Carmo pulled out his bag then and began to go through it. "I brought a few loaves of bread, some rolls, and some pastries for us all." He looked up at Hanne then. "I didn't think to bring anything else."

Evren opened a big cloth and spread it out on the ground before them. "I have dried fruit and three kinds of cheese. I brought some apples as well. You're all welcome to it."

Padma tilted her head to one side. "Perhaps if we pool all the food together and just eat a little of it each day we'll be able to make good meals and not be hungry along the journey. We've mostly brought different things. I think it will work out okay, though we don't have much meat, but the rest is all right. I have eggs from our henhouse." She showed them how carefully she had wrapped them all so that they wouldn't break. They piled all their food together and gazed at it with no small amount of concern.

"Do you think it will be enough?" Carmo asked, realizing that it was much less even cumulatively than he had thought that it might be when they were talking about it all.

Hanne bit at her lower lip and then raised her eyes to her friends. "I think this is going to make some scant meals."

Evren scowled. "It's not going to be enough for all of us! Someone will have to go back for more!"

Padma's face grew stern. "No one is going back. We'll just have to tighten our belts. We'll make do."

"We won't have to tighten them too much because the forest will give us what we need to get by fairly well." Amias said with a sigh.

All four of the other friends gasped and jerked their heads up to look at him. None of them had seen him coming or heard him at all. "Amias!" They chorused in surprise.

"You came!" Carmo grinned, as did the rest of the group.

Amias nodded and bent slightly to set his sack down on the ground near them. "I wasn't going to, but I knew that you would be better off with me and I couldn't just stay back and leave you to the mountain on your own. We're friends, and though I have no interest in the Wish Weaver, I do have an interest in all of you. What kind of friend would I be if I didn't come to help?" He gave them a smile and laid three dead rabbits on the ground.

Amias turned away then and they watched as he disappeared into the darkness and then came back shortly with a large log of wood that had once been part of a fallen tree. He arranged it carefully on the fire and then added some more shorter, smaller pieces around it.

"We'll need a bigger fire for safety and warmth. It's going to get colder in the early hours of the morning, and none of the animals will come near with a big fire." He got to work then cooking the rabbits he'd brought so they could all have a hot meal.

"I've brought my traps and fishing line with me, so we'll have plenty to eat, and the forest grows a lot of food that we can harvest." He talked as he cooked, and the scent of the warming meat reminded them all just how hungry they really were.

They ate together and talked a little, but their weariness at the wee hour, along with their full bellies, sent them all off to sleep. When they awoke, the smell of cooking eggs and meat greeted them, along with a strange scent they had never smelled before.

Amias was working over the remnants of their fire from the night before, and his friends were grateful for it right away.

"You made breakfast for us?" Carmo asked with a smile, pushing himself up from the blanket he'd slept in.

"We're going to take it in turns to prepare meals, but I thought I'd do breakfast this morning, yes." He gave some food to the boy and then handed him a cup with steaming liquid in it.

"What's this?" Carmo asked curiously as he peered into the cup.

"It's nettle tea. It's good for you. Drink up, you'll need it." Amias handed cups of the strange smelling tea to the rest of his friends and they sniffed suspiciously but did as he bid them and drank it.

When their meal was done and their campsite was undone, they loaded their sacks onto their shoulders and followed Amias up the slight slope of the mountain base. The further they hiked, the steeper the terrain grew in most places, save for a few areas where there were meadows and ponds.

They hadn't gone too far when Padma stopped in her tracks and raised her head high at full attention. Everyone else stopped and looked at her. She turned her head slowly and looked around.

"What is it?" Evren asked worriedly.

She furrowed her brow. "Can you hear that? It's a... a rushing sort of sound. I can't tell what it is."

Amias spoke evenly. "It's a river that comes off of a waterfall further up the mountain. It's swift, it's deep, and it's very cold. There's a bridge up ahead where we can get to the other side."

Hanne's eyes went wide. "I'm so glad that you decided to come along, Amias. I don't know how we'd have made it without you."

He only smiled and continued heading toward the sound of the rapid river with his friends following closely behind him. The roar of the crashing water grew louder as they approached it, and when they got to the small rickety bridge that spanned the river, they all stopped and stared at it.

"Do you think we can make it across that safely?" Evren asked, peering at the time worn rope and half rotted wooden planks that stretched out before them swaying haphazardly over the thundering current deep in the canyon below.

Amias studied the bridge and nodded. "Yes, if we're very careful we'll make it. Follow me and step only where I step. I've been over this bridge a few times, but it's been a little while. Let's watch out for one another and whatever you do, don't let go of the rope."

~ 45 ~

He went first, testing each plank with pressure from his foot before he stepped on it, mindfully avoiding this one and that one, tentatively making his way across, with the line of his friends behind him walking in his precise path. They all held fast and nearly held their breath as they tiptoed step by step toward the opposite bank.

Amias reached it and immediately turned to hold his hand out to each of his friends as they came near to him, pulling them all to safety one by one. When Evren, who came last, fell to his knees on the grass with gratitude, they all breathed a sigh of relief.

"We made it! We all made it!" Carmo half laughed and half sighed as his shoulders fell with the release of his anxiety.

"We did make it. Let's keep going." Amias said, looking up at the sun to determine how much daylight they had left before they'd have to make camp again that night. "We want to go as far as we can each day so that the journey is short."

The friends turned and began to head into the thick wall of trees around them, but they hadn't gotten far when a piercing scream sounded and all of them startled, their eyes searching each other.

"What was that?" Carmo asked worriedly.

"It sounded like a scream…" Evren replied, trailing off and furrowing his brow as he looked over his shoulder where they had come from. Amias was already racing past him back through the trees they had just entered. Everyone followed him at a run.

They reached the bank of the river and Hanne cried out loudly, covering her hand over her mouth as Padma swiftly grabbed her arms, holding her in place.

"Petia! Oh no! Petia!" Hanne's voice was filled with terror. Halfway along the old rope bridge was her younger sister. Petia was hanging onto what was left of a broken plank, her lower body fallen through the bridge and her torso and arms locked onto the scrap of wood that had broken beneath her step. She was smudged head to toe in dirt and her dress was torn in places. Her eyes were wide with fear as she screamed and cried to the group on the bank.

Amias lit over the bridge like lightning, zig zagging his way from one step to the next, nearly slipping once himself before he regained his footing and finally reached the little girl. Hanne tried to tug herself out of Padma's grasp, but Padma held her fast.

"Stay here, Amias can get her. If you go you might fall through too, and we can't have you both in danger. Stay here where it's safe and let him do this." Padma's voice was deceptively calm and steady, and Hanne listened to her and stayed on the bank though she was trembling and weeping a torrent.

Amias knelt down carefully, one plank away from Petia. He looked directly at her and spoke evenly, trying to calm the girl a little even though he was far from calm inside. "Petia, look at me… look right at my eyes and don't look away. Just keep looking at me." He was stern though caring. She met his stare and kicked her feet, panic flooding her.

"I'm falling! I'm falling in the water!" She sobbed, her breath short as she gasped and flailed.

Amias held his hands out to her. "You have to calm down; if you keep kicking you're going to fall. You have to hold still so I can help you. You can do this. Trust me. Just hold very still and I'll reach out and get you. I'm not going to let you fall, but you must help me, okay? Stay still. Do you trust me?"

Petia nodded, her tear stained cheeks flushed hotly, and she stopped struggling though she whined loudly with fear as she watched him. He nodded and encouraged her. "That's good! That's very good! Now, I need you to take a deep breath and keep your eyes on me."

She tried to do as he told her to, though her breath didn't go very deep. He braced himself against the only part of the bridge that was stable under him in that place, and slowly he leaned forward with one hand fisted around the rope beside him and one hand reaching out to her. He drew near enough to her that his head was beside hers, and he wrapped his free arm around her back and waist.

"I need you to put one arm around my neck. I've got a hold of you, but you have to take hold of me, too. Reach one arm around my neck, and then when you've got me good, put your other arm around my neck too, and I'll pull you up." He told her as steadily as he could. His heart was racing faster than it ever had and he had never been more afraid than he was at that moment, but it was his fear that made him strong and he refused to let her see anything but strength in his eyes.

Petia shook her head quickly. "No! No! I can't let go!" She insisted, but he stopped her.

"You have to! Petia, you must try! It's the only way! Now let go with one arm only and hug it around my neck. You can do this! Be brave!" She looked uncertain, but he urged her again. "Do it now!" He raised his voice and in that moment she was startled and as a reaction to his insistence, she let go of the wood and closed one arm tightly around his neck.

"You did it! You did it…" He breathed a half sigh and tried to smile at her a little. "I've got you and you've got me, now all you have to do is let go with the other arm and hug that one around my neck too. You can do it, and then we'll be able to get over the bridge. Come on. You can do this!"

Feeling some small semblance of courage from her first success, she gritted her teeth and flung her other arm around his neck as snugly as she could. Hanne called out to them from the opposite bank, but Amias spoke into Petia's ear with his even tone.

"Close your eyes. I'm going to pull you up and you must stay still so I can get you free. The easiest way for you to do that is to close your eyes and think of Hanne. She's right behind us, just on the other side there, and we can get to her if you stay still and hold on tight."

"Okay." Her voice was little more than a whimper. She closed her eyes and held on with all her might.

Gently and carefully, he used every ounce of strength within him to lift her body up and pull her toward him until he could stand up. When his feet were flat on a plank, he felt it creak and groan beneath the weight of them both.

Amias closed his own eyes for a moment and wished with everything in him that they could make it back safely to their friends on the other side. Taking a deep breath, he reopened his eyes and turned, taking one meticulously placed step after another while his friends looked on breathlessly, holding one another's hands as they waited.

Just as he had pulled all of them to safety when they had crossed the bridge the first time, four pairs of hands stretched out and grabbed at Amias and Petia the moment that they were in reach, dragging both of them onto the foundation of grass at their feet.

Hanne and Petia locked their arms around each other and wept with relief as the rest of the friends comforted each other in gratitude. At last Hanne let Petia go and looked at her sternly.

"What on earth are you doing here? I told you to stay at home!" Frustration and grief colored Hanne's voice, and Petia didn't miss the look of disapproval in her sister's eyes.

"I couldn't stay behind. I wanted to be with you!" She whimpered quietly, staring up with a sad gaze at her sister.

Hanne only gazed at her sister for a moment before sighing heavily and holding her close once more. "You shouldn't be here, Petia. You shouldn't be here at all, but we can't turn back now. I guess you'll have to come with us." Hanne looked up at her friends and they all gave her a nod of approval.

"Hanne…" Petia gasped worriedly, looking up at her sister again, "my side hurts."

Hanne's eyes widened, and she stared at the young girl's side, where Petia was holding her hands over her ribs. Her dress was ripped from the wooden plank she had fallen through, and Hanne could see where her skin had been scraped and was bleeding just a little bit.

Padma sank down to the ground beside Petia and placed her hand on the girl's shoulder. "Lay back on the grass and let me have a look." Her mother was the village healer and she helped her from time to time. She knew a fair amount about healing, but her mother did most of the work.

Padma moved her fingers over Petia's side gently, pressing here and there as she examined the girl. Petia cried out a few times and finally Padma turned to Hanne with a serious expression on her face.

"She has three broken ribs." Padma spoke in a low voice. "There's nothing that can be done about it, except to wrap them. She's going to have a hard time walking with us and sleeping, but she will heal. It's just not going to be easy for her on this journey."

Hanne gave her a grateful nod and held Petia's hand as Padma reached into her bag for a long strap of material and then wrapped it around Petia's torso tightly. When the young girl was ready to go, they helped her get to her feet and then they set off together again up the mountain, though there was an air of apprehension among them that hadn't been there before.

Their pace was slowed considerably, but together they traveled until Amias stopped and looked around them at the thick trees, and he turned to look back at the ground that they had covered to that point.

"What is it?" Evren asked curiously, following his friend's eyes and trying to see what Amias was looking at.

"This is the furthest I've been from the village. I do not know anything about what may come after this, so we must all be wary of the forest around us. We are not alone, not at all. Everyone keep a watch as we go." He was more on guard than any of them had ever seen him, and the gravity of their situation was impressed upon each one of the friends.

"How will we find our way then?" Carmo asked with a nuance of confusion unhidden in his voice.

Hanne looked up the slope of ground before them and shrugged. "I guess we go up and we head for the peak. We just keep going bit by bit until we can get there and find the Wish Weaver."

Carmo pressed his lips together with a look of unease and gave her a nod. Together they all walked, sometimes talking, but most often going in silence. They kept their eyes on the forest around them which was easy to do, as none of them had ever seen anything like it before.

The familiarity of the trees and sparseness of the edge of the woods near the village had transitioned into massive thick old trees which stood like giants guarding the mountain they were slowly making their way up. The trees were covered in moss and growth and it amazed them that every trunk, limb, and branch was hidden in layers upon layers of life; green, yellow, brown, budding, expanding, growing, dying.

Such density all around them on every natural part of the forest, save for the forest floor, made the space around them seem smaller, as if the woods were crowding in on them and closing them in a dark and strange embrace.

Even the light was different as it filtered through the thickening foliage, growing dimmer the further they went, and they noticed that the air grew more still as the trees held back the wind. The space around them was quieter as less birdsong sounded and the trees and leaves barely moved.

The weighted quietness made it easier to hear things around them, and the group stopped short when Amias froze and held his hands out, blocking them. Blinking at him, Evren tilted his head.

"What is it?" he asked curiously. "Why are we stopping?"

"Can you hear that?" Amias asked, peering around them into the trees behind them.

"I don't hear anything." Carmo answered, staring at the forest.

"Me either." Evren replied, gazing back at Amias. "What did you hear?"

"Wolves." Amias answered gravely. "I heard wolves and they're close behind us!"

Chapter Four

Out on a Limb

All of his friends stared at Amias with wide eyes for one full second as they digested his words and their meaning and then panic flooded their faces. Amias grabbed Petia's hand. "Quick! Up into the trees or they'll be able to get us!"

Not another word was spoken as the children scrambled up the nearest tree trunk, thick and tall. Padma and Amias worked together to get Petia up as Evren and Hanne helped Carmo. The little girl was brave as she worked her way up the tree, holding tightly to knots and branches as she winced in pain but didn't cry out. The only evidence of it were the tears in her eyes and on her red cheeks.

The growth along the tree trunk gave them footholds as they all made their way up, reaching to help one another and get to the lowest branches just as a big pack of wolves ran up the hill and encircled the tree.

The beasts snarled and barked, their black eyes glittering with nothing but ravenous hunger as they leapt at the feet of the children, desperate to reach them. Each one of the friends had just managed to make it up to the lowest lying limbs of the tree, but it was immediately clear that even that height wouldn't be quite enough to stay safely out of the reach of the wolves as they wove in between each other and tried to claw their way up the trunk.

Amias looked sharply at his friends and raised his voice above the growling and barking of their attackers. "All of you! Up! Up higher! We can't stay this close to the ground!"

One by one the friends clambered up, their fingers gripping the smaller branches, their arms holding fast to the limbs, until they were far enough out of the way that they couldn't be reached.

It wasn't until then that any of them even dared to breathe, and they looked at each other with terrified eyes.

"Are you all right?" Hanne asked, reaching for her sister with a firm hand.

Petia nodded and wiped tears from her cheeks. "I'm so scared!" She barely spoke as her small body trembled.

Carmo was staring down at the wolves who glared furiously up at them, jumping up the tree as far as they could, determined to get their prey. "They almost got us." He gasped in a low voice filled with disbelief. He shook his head slowly, as if he couldn't comprehend the fact that he was where he was at that moment, facing mortal danger; it was the farthest he had ever been from the sweet, slow routine of his life.

"They did get me!" Evren cried out anxiously, examining the leg of his pants. One of the wolves had closed its teeth around the hem of the material, narrowly missing Evren's leg, and shredded his fine clothes. The pants were torn roughly from the hem to Evren's knee. He ran his fingers over the cloth again and again, fretting over the state of it.

"Look at this! Look at it! I wore my best clothes for the Wish Weaver! My very best, so that I could impress her and show her just how good I would look in better clothes, to show her just how much I need my wish to come true and look at this! I'm a shambles!" He began to weep as he leaned his head back against the trunk of the tree and moaned miserably.

Amias reached his hand out and closed it gently over Padma's shoulder. She had grown pale and still, staring down at the wolves as if in a trance. He spoke her name softly, as quietly as a prayer, and she didn't blink. He closed his fingers a little more around her shoulder to draw her back to them again and spoke her name once more.

"Padma... Padma." His dark eyes searched her stony face with concern.

She did not respond to him. Hanne looked over at them as she held Petia close to her heart, her arms wrapped around her sister in a comforting embrace. "Padma!" She called out gently. Amias gave the girl's shoulder a squeeze and finally Padma blinked and turned her head slowly to face him.

"Are you all right?" He asked, knowing full well what she had been through and that she must be having a much harder time with their attack than any of the others.

She choked back a sob and shook her head. She couldn't even speak. He nodded and closed an arm around her shoulder, giving her a strong hug. "We're going to make it. We're going to be all right." Padma only buried her face in his neck and wept quietly.

"They can't reach us," Carmo said as he sat huddled on his tree limb, "but they aren't leaving!"

"They won't leave for a long while. We're treed, and they know that we can't escape. They will wait there until we come down or fall down." Amias told his young friend, and Carmo drew in a sharp breath.

"We're going to die here!" He cried out in terror.

Amias knit his brow and studied the wolves for a moment before looking around them. "There has to be a way out for us. There has to be something. Give me a moment." He spoke evenly. Studying the area they were in, he considered their realistic options. If they went down the tree the wolves would get them, and he knew that the wolves would not leave. The pack continued to circle the base of the tree, howling and growling, raring to get to their meal.

Pressing his lips together in a thin line, Amias searched all around them, looking at the fat limbs that they were huddled upon, and the other trees that grew thick near the one they were all perched in.

"I think I've got an idea." He announced to them in a curious tone. Every one of his friends locked their eyes on him in desperate hope. He pointed to the limb he was sitting on and then raised his hand, following the path of it as it reached to the tree beside them.

"These trees grow so close together that the limbs touch. If we go one by one, we can crawl along the limbs from one tree to the next. Now, the wolves are going to follow us, but I can hear water up ahead. If we can get to the water, we might be able to jump down into it and swim away from the wolves. They won't follow us into moving water." He sounded only moderately hopeful, but it was the only chance that any of them had.

Amias went first, testing the tree limbs to be sure that they could hold his weight, knowing that most of his friends weighed about the same as he did or were lighter, and very carefully, he made his way from the place where he, Padma, Hanne, and Petia were rooted.

Crawling on his belly and using his arms and legs to inch along the length of wood, he managed to get to the limb of the next tree, and when he was safely there, he called back to the others. "Come on! All of you can make it!"

Hanne looked at her sister. "I know with your injuries that you're going to have a hard time with this, so I want you to lay on my back when I crawl over, and just hold on to my neck." Petia shook her head.

"I can't do it!" She whimpered, but then Evren who had worked his way to the spot where Hanne and Petia were, comforted her.

"You can make it. We're all going to make it. Just close your eyes, hold on tight, and don't look down." He sounded sure of himself, though Hanne thought he looked more miserable than she had ever seen him. She was still grateful for his words of encouragement to her sister.

"Thank you, Evren." She sighed heavily. He nodded and looked over at Padma, waiting to see what she was going to do. She took a deep breath and with mechanical movements, she wrapped herself around the limb the way that Amias had, and she inched along the branch until she crossed over into the neighboring tree.

The wolves grew panicked and confused, uncertain which tree they should be running at, and angry because their prey was moving out of reach. Padma was barely breathing by the time she reached Amias, and when she got to him, she nearly collapsed against the trunk of the tree where it met the branch she was on.

With the jaws of the beasts snapping as they growled and leapt up as far as they could, Evren helped Petia onto

Hanne's back, and Hanne gritted her teeth and held on as tight as she could for both of their lives. Keeping her eyes on Amias, whose hand was outstretched to her, she crawled over to him, focusing with all her might on his encouraging words rather than on the barks and howls of the fierce wolves just below them.

When she made it to Amias, he helped Petia first, and she scuttled over to where Padma was pressed close to the trunk, then they waved at Evren and Carmo. Evren made it across quickly, complaining the whole way about how the method for their crossing over the wood was destroying what was left of his clothes. Once he was safely over to the next tree, he began dusting the moss and twigs off of his fine clothes immediately and bemoaning the state of his dress.

Carmo was the last to cross over and he went the slowest, only able to go inch by inch as the fear of falling to the ravenous wolves below gripped him in its icy clutches. He kept closing his eyes tightly and trying to tell himself not to look down, and his friends did all that they could to urge him on, but still he could barely make himself move.

With everyone save Padma, who was closing her eyes and burying her face against the tree trunk, calling to Carmo and encouraging him, he finally made it across to them, out of breath and pink faced, wishing that he hadn't come along on the journey.

"The wolves followed us!" Petia cried out, staring at the ground below the new tree they were in, her eyes roving back and forth over the animals which weren't any further away from them than they had been in the last tree.

"They're going to stay with us until we get to a place where they won't follow, or can't follow. We're going to have to keep going from tree to tree until we can get away from them." Amias told her sympathetically.

The friends groaned and sighed with exasperation at Amias' words, but he tried to comfort them. "We'll go, and we'll keep going. We'll help each other and at some point, we will get to a situation that will work for us. I believe that. I believe in all of you, and in us working together to make it through."

Carmo plucked up his courage as he heard Amias speaking, and he nodded, looking at the others. "If Amias thinks that we can do this, then I think so too. We've already outsmarted the wolves this far, so let's keep going. Let's try to get as far as we can until we can get away from them!"

The others agreed, and so the group of friends continued their way, going slowly from tree to tree, along one branch and then another while keeping as far above the ground as they could, and the wolves followed them, growing hungrier and angrier as their prey continued to elude them.

At long last the friends came to a deep and swift moving creek that was more than twelve feet across. Amias finally breathed a sigh of relief as he looked at the branches that stretched so far over the water that they connected in the middle to trees from the other side of the creek. The branches formed a great arch over the water for quite a distance.

"This is it!" He cried out to them with tremendous hope. "We're not going to have to get into the water. This limb is tangled up with the branches from the trees over the water on the other side. If we can make it across this creek, the wolves won't have any way to follow us. We'll be able to get down on the ground and walk again. There's no way for them to cross here!"

His friends heaved great sighs of relief as a few of them managed small smiles to him in gratitude. Petia was terrified and Carmo looked as if he was just as scared as she was.

"But what if we fall off of the branches into the water?" She wailed with fear.

Amias shook his head. "We made it this far without falling, we'll make it across this the same way. We look ahead, we don't look down, and I'll take you on my back this time if you want me to."

She nodded and clutched her small hands together tightly. "Yes, thank you."

Slinging the length of rope he'd been carrying off of his torso, Amias carefully tied it around each of their waists until they were all connected at short lengths one by one to the rope. The beginning of the rope was cinched around his waist, and Padma insisted that the end of it be tied to her waist as she was one of the strongest swimmers in their group.

They prepared to go across and Amias went with Evren and Hanne right behind him. One by one, save for Amias who carried Petia on his back, they made their way over the tree limbs as the wolves danced in rage at the bank of the creek, howling furiously as they realized they would not be able to track their prey any longer.

Amias had never been as afraid as he was traversing the tree limbs over the water that rushed and rolled wildly below them. Though the water was clear, it was so deep that none of them could see the bottom of the creek bed, and all of them did their best to keep their eyes level and focused on the tree that they would reach once they got to the other side.

Moving slowly, they all made their way, calling back to one another here and there to make sure that they were all still safe and moving. At long last they reached the far side where the tree trunks were even wider than the trees had been behind them. Panting, they huddled together at the base of the limb, reaching for each other's hands and shoulders as small smiles of triumph formed over their faces.

"We made it!" Carmo cried out with tremendous relief, and the others joined in with their own gratitude for the success of their plan.

"It wasn't that difficult." Evren shrugged and Hanne laughed at him and shook her head.

"It was really difficult, but we tried, and together we made it." She heaved a sigh and reached her arm around Petia, pulling her near. "Now we just need to get down and get going again."

Padma looked back at the opposite bank where the wolves were still pacing furiously and howling in anger at the group. "We just made it. I can't believe we got away from them." She spoke in a low voice, her body still trembling slightly.

Amias let out a big breath. "Well we did make it, and now we need to get out of this tree and get away from the creek. We need to find a safe place to camp for the night."

Amias dropped down the length of the tree trunk with ease, looking back up at his friends and offering them help as they followed him down carefully. Once they were all on the ground, they gave one last swift look at the wolves who barked and growled at them from the opposite shore, and they hurried further into the forest to put some distance between the predators and themselves.

Carmo looked around and lowered a brow in suspicion. "It's strange here." He said almost under his breath.

Padma turned her gaze to him. "How so?"

He pressed his lips together into a thin line as he considered his answer before he spoke. "It's quiet here, but it's not silent. I can hear things, but I can't see anything that might be making the noises around us."

"The whole forest is like that." Amias smiled lightly at him over his shoulder. "You'll get used to it the longer we're here."

Petia shivered as she peered at the dimly lit space that seemed to close in around them. "I hope we aren't out here for very long. I want to go home."

Hanne sighed. "I wish you hadn't come. You wouldn't be hurt, and I would know that you were safe."

Petia gave her sister a plaintive look. "But I had to be with you! I was scared that you'd be so far away!"

Hanne nodded. "I understand, I just wish you'd stayed behind. This journey is no place for you."

Carmo's expression darkened. "I'm not sure that it's a place for any of us."

Evren piped up then with an encouraging tone. "Just remember why we're going! We're going to have our deepest wishes granted! Imagine! That in itself is a reason to go! We'll be fine. We'll get to her and make our wishes and then go right back home again."

"I'm have no wish to make." Amias stated evenly.

Evren leveled his gaze at him. "Then you could wish us home so that we don't have to make the trek back, if you're not going to come up with your own wish."

"I'm not making a wish. There's something about it that seems wrong to me. I told you this. You can't get something for nothing. It's so unlikely that there's some old woman out in the woods granting wishes freely to one and all." He shook his head and slowed his pace as he studied the woods around them.

"Well I believe that she's there and that she'll grant our wishes to us." Padma replied, giving them both a smile.

"I believe it, too." Hanne chimed in. "Otherwise what are we even going for?"

Amias stopped and gazed closely around them for a long moment.

"What is it?" Carmo asked with a note of worry in his voice and concern in his eyes.

"Nothing, I just think we should stop and set up camp here for the night. It looks like a good place. There's a small meadow there, ringed thick with trees. We'll have some protection from the weather that way, and a comfortable place to sleep." He led them to the intimate clearing and turned to Padma and Evren. "Help me find wood for a fire, please." Then he looked over at Hanne and Carmo. "If you two don't mind, please begin to prepare a meal for us." He glanced at Petia as he handed his water pouch to her.

"You need to sit and rest. You've been moving too much. Drink all the water in this. I'll refill it soon enough." With that, he handed the water pouch to her and she dutifully did as he said.

Amias, Evren, and Padma all spread out in search of firewood and it took them nearly no time at all to return to the small meadow with armloads of it. Soon enough Amias had a good fire going with flames burning big and bright as the smoke rose in a trail and reached up into the darkening night.

He cooked fish for them, and they ate some vegetables and baked rolls. When they were full they curled up close together in a ring and pulled their blankets up around themselves. Most of them fell asleep, but Amias laid in the thick grass and stared up at the brilliant stars in the black velvet sky, considering their journey and what might come ahead, and how they might get back to the village. He had come along on the journey to look after his friends, and when he had set out from the village to travel with them he hadn't quite realized just how big a responsibility that might become. The weight of it stayed in his mind and he could not stop thinking of it.

Late in the night, sleep finally took him, and all the children dreamt until the light of morning and a clinging mist woke them gradually from their slumber. Amias stoked the fire and began to prepare the breakfast meal as the others rose.

Carmo went to Amias to help him and he reached into one of his bags to get some of the pastries he'd brought along. With a gasp, he froze and stared hard at the bag.

Amias turned to him, seeing his surprise. "What is it?"

Carmo pulled his bag open wide and began to rustle around in it. "I… I can't find the pastries I brought."

"Are you certain that's where you left them?" Amias asked lightly.

Carmo nodded. "Yes, it's right where I left them. They were here, right in this bag and now they're gone. All of them are gone!" He gushed in astonishment. Looking up at Amias, he frowned.

"What do you think happened to them? Did they fall out along the way? Perhaps as we were climbing through the trees?" Amias considered thoughtfully.

With a shake of his head, Carmo looked around at his friends. "No. Nothing fell out of the bag. The pastries were there last night when we were making camp. I nearly pulled them out for dinner but decided to save them for breakfast and now they're gone. That means someone sneaked into the bag and took them to eat!"

Disappointment colored the young boy's face as he turned to gaze at his friends in disbelief.

"I didn't touch your bag." Evren shot at him defensively.

"Nor I." Padma added with a shake of her head.

Hanne lifted her chin. "Petia and I were sleeping on the other side of the fire. We didn't come anywhere near you last night."

"Well someone took them!" Carmo challenged them. "They're gone! Who was it?" He demanded, his cheeks growing pink with frustration as his eyes glistened.

Amias held his hands up. "Stop please! Listen..." They all turned to look at him and he spoke with a calm voice. "Is any of the other food missing?"

Each one investigated their bags and shook their heads. "Everything is here." Padma replied, opening wide the bag in which most of their food had been pooled together. Each of them double checked their own sacks. Amias paced a few steps as he rubbed his thumb over his chin.

"There's nothing missing but the pastries." He murmured in a soft voice and then he stopped pacing and knelt at his sack, pulling out one of his traps.

Carmo tilted his head curiously. "What are you doing?"

Amias spoke as he looked up at his young friend. "Well if it wasn't any of us, then logically we can assume that it was someone or something else." He reached for one of the rolls that was left over from the night before. "We know that only the pastries are gone, so I'm going to set a trap with a baked roll and we'll see if something takes the bait."

He set the trap near the base of a tree at the edge of the meadow and they all returned to the fire, facing their backs to the trap, eating their breakfasts and talking purposefully about anything else.

A short while later, just as they were finishing their meal, a piercing howl sounded from near the tree and Amias stood immediately and turned toward the place where the trap had been laid. "I think we might have something." He said quietly.

With even, steady steps, he headed toward the edge of the meadow and his friends followed along closely behind him, their eyes wide with curiosity.

When they reached the tree, they all stopped short and stared, and Amias went to the trap. Stuck there inside it was a small being no taller than Amias' knees. It had features like a human; a head with a face and a wild tangle of dark salt and pepper hair that stuck out all over from beneath a strange looking cap of large autumn leaves fitted snugly on its head. Its body was small with two arms and two legs, hands and feet. He was dressed in what looked like tree bark that had been rubbed soft the way that leather could be, and the strange material was shaped into pants that were held onto his body over his shoulders with straps of lightly woven straw. He had a shirt that looked as if it were made of thistle down and might have been white at one time long before then. Upon his small feet were worn brown boots turned up at the toe with a short cuff around the ankle.

The little being glared at the group of friends and then let out a loud howl as he tried unsuccessfully to free himself from Amias' trap. Carmo leaned a little closer and eyed the little old man creature.

"Look at the crumbs in its beard! It ate the pastries!" Carmo's expression grew sharp as he accused the small being.

Hanne covered her mouth with her hand and turned her stunned face from the little being back to Amias. "What are we going to do with it?"

Carmo stood up and staunchly crossed his arms over his chest. "We keep it in the trap. If we let it out, it will steal more of our food!"

"We can't keep it in the trap!" Petia came to the creature's defense. "That would be cruel! We must let it go!"

Evren shook his head. "I agree with Carmo. We should keep it in the trap."

Padma sighed and fretted over it, liking the way that the diminutive chubby being looked. She planted her hands on her hips. "I don't like that. I don't think we should keep it in the trap. What if it dies in there? We're leaving. It will need food and water. I don't want to kill it." She considered their predicament for a moment as the creature watched her, its eyes darting back and forth between the friends as it kept its mouth clamped shut.

Kneeling a safe but short distance from the trap, she peered at him. "What if we leave it in the trap now and then release it after we've been to see the Wish Weaver?"

Hanne touched Padma's shoulder. "We don't know how long we'll be gone or if we'll even come back this way. We have no way of knowing how much time it will really take us to get to the Wish Weaver. I think we're going to have to make a decision right now as to whether we keep it in the trap or let it go."

Evren furrowed his brow. "Why should we let it go? It could be dangerous! We don't even know what it is!"

The creature had been listening to the entire discussion and at that point, it spoke to them with a gruff and impatient voice. "*It* is a hobgoblin, and its name is Mr. Trumbles."

Every pair of eyes was locked on the little hobgoblin as he continued to speak. "I know the way to the Wish Weaver. I don't think ye do. If ye free me from the trap, I will make an accord with ye. I will lead ye to the Wish Weaver. All I ask is me freedom and a share of the food ye have. Especially those pastries. What do ye say?"

Taken by surprise at his capability to communicate and his intelligence, they were left speechless for a long moment, until Amias faced his friends and spoke up. "I say we vote on it. Do we hire Mr. Trumbles as our guide for the price of a share of the meals, or do we leave him here? All for taking him along?"

Amias raised his own hand and Padma, Hanne, and Petia followed suit. Carmo pouted darkly, but finally he raised his hand slightly. Evren crossed his arms over his chest defiantly and lifted his chin in refusal.

"He comes with us then." Amias stated as he knelt close to the trap and freed the hobgoblin. Mr. Trumbles pushed the trap away from himself the moment he was out of it and he gave it a kick before looking at everyone but Evren.

"Ye'll never make it without me, so it's good ye'll be having me along." Mr. Trumbles told them with a somber tone. "Pack up yer bags and let's go. It's a long way off."

Chapter Five

A Feast of Fools

The band of friends in the company of their new guide trekked through the forest as they ascended the mountain, talking as they made their way. Petia and Hanne were so curious about their new companion that they were more focused on him and on getting to know him than they were on the trip for a short while.

"Mr. Trumbles," Hanne cocked an eyebrow at him, "are you sure that you know the way to the Wish Weaver?"

He gave her a sidelong look of slight annoyance. "Aye, I know the way."

Petia piped up then. "Meesta Trumbows, I've never heard of a hobgoblin before. Can you do magic?" A smile of fascination spread over her face at the idea of it.

The corners of the hobgoblin's mouth turned up a bit as he lowered his eyelids in a pleased sort of expression. "We do some bits of magic around the forest. Just bits. Nothing big or fancy, mind ye."

The young girl's eyes went wide with admiration. Padma walked near them then and spoke up as well. "I know of hobgoblin magic. You do good work in the forest, keeping it safe and helping things to grow, don't you?" She eyed Mr. Trumbles with interest.

The hobgoblin nodded. "Aye, most of us do."

"Not all of you?" Hanne asked with a frown of confusion.

Mr. Trumbles continued to move swiftly through the forest, much more quickly than any of them had guessed he might. "Most of us." He reiterated without looking over at her.

"I've heard that your kind can see far in the night, and that you can hear better than most creatures in the woods." Evren called out to Mr. Trumbles. "Is that true?"

The little being nodded as he hobbled along. "Aye."

"Well then I'm glad that you're along with us, Sir." Petia beamed at him and he glanced over at her and gave her a wink and a smile.

The young girl looked up at her sister then. "I'm hungry." It had been quite a few hours since they had eaten breakfast and broken their camp to continue the journey. Padma agreed.

"I'm hungry too."

"Me too." Hanne sighed.

Amias frowned slightly. "I know you're all feeling a little hungry, but when we crested that hill a little while ago I think I saw a place up ahead that would be good for us to camp at for the night. If we can continue to press forward now maybe we can have a little bit of a longer rest this evening when we stop."

Petia pouted and Evren gave Amias a nod. "I think we should press on as well. I want to get there soon. The sooner we get our wishes granted, the sooner we can get back to the village and be home."

"What's that?" Padma asked as she slowed in her walking and then came to a full stop. The others paused to look over at her.

"What's what?" Amias asked, narrowing his eyes some as he gazed around them. He hadn't seen or heard anything out of the ordinary.

Padma pointed to a small glowing light that looked no bigger than a bumblebee. "That... that little glowing... thing." She tilted her head as she watched it floating through the air in an almost lazy sort of way just out of her reach at about the level of her heart.

"Oh! I see it!" Petia chimed in. "Look, there are more of them!" She pointed just above a nearby bush where five or six more were floating around near each other, hovering delicately in the air.

"They're so pretty!" Hanne smiled, reaching her hand out to see if she could touch one of them. "I wonder what they are!"

Mr. Trumbles hurried his short legs and he came to her side and looked up at the growing number of the glowing lights. "They're Charmers. They're no good! Best to stay away from them. Let's go."

He turned to leave but the girls were entranced and Evren joined them, staring at the lights. Amias sighed and walked toward where his friends had gathered. "I think Mr. Trumbles is right. I think we should continue on."

"I like them! I want to watch them a bit longer! I've never seen anything like them!" Evren smiled, dazzled by the lights.

"Charmers are bad!" Mr. Trumbles said again. "They'll charm ye right to yer death!"

"These things couldn't be bad!" Padma waved her hand in the air dismissively. "Look how pretty they are!"

The glowing golden lights began to grow in number and they seemed to nuzzle the children, floating around them in a sort of embrace. A few of the Charmers bobbed before the children and began to float away, and Petia took a few steps to follow them. "I think they want us to go this way!" She grinned, watching them.

A few more Charmers formed into a small stream and looked as if they were leading a trail, circling around the group and then breaking off into the forest slowly, almost as if they were lassoing the group and pulling them further into the trees and away from the direction they had all been traveling in.

Amias and Mr. Trumbles shared a frustrated look, but there was no stopping the others who were enchanted with the Charmers and were happy to follow them wherever they led.

"Would you look at that! What a sight!" Evren cried out just as the others came up right behind him and gaped in awe at what they saw. Just before them in a small clearing in the wood was a great banquet table set finer than any of them had ever seen in their lives. Abundant trays of delicious looking food were set about on a crisp white linen, and tall taper candles were tipped with dancing flames. Golden plates and goblets shone, and fresh flowers filled crystal vases. All around the long table there were cushioned chairs set back just waiting for any guest to enjoy the feast.

"My goodness! I've never seen anything like it!" Padma gasped as she walked to the back of one chair and put her hands upon it.

"Do you think it would be all right if we sat at the table and ate?" Hanne asked hopefully, looking around at her friends. The Charmers glowed ever brighter and encircled them all, swirling and spiraling through the air and around the table.

"Of course we can! This is what our new friends the Charmers have brought us here to do! Let's sit and have a meal! We were just saying how hungry we are. We need a good meal and a rest. Come! Let's all sit down and eat! There's room for everyone!" He pulled a chair out and sat in it, and the others followed suit, save for Mr. Trumbles who refused to get close to the table, and Amias who was just at the edge of the clearing.

"I don't think we should be doing this!" Amias called out to his friends. "What would a feast so fine as this be doing out in the forest rather than in a lord's manor or a castle? This isn't right! I don't think that this is for us! Please, come back away from the table!"

Evren scoffed. "Oh doubter! You never believe in anything good! Think of all that you miss by being so suspicious all the time! Just look at this! It's wonderful! Let go of your worry for once and join us!"

His friends were already reaching for the food and drinks waiting for them. He took a few steps toward the table with his hands outstretched hoping to stop them, when everything began to change.

The cup in Petia's hand began to disappear as did the fork full of food in Evren's hand, and the apple in Hanne's fingers. Padma gasped as the table before them and everything on it began to vanish, like a fading mist. It all disappeared as they watched in surprise, and the last thing to go were the chairs.

Instead of finding themselves sitting in seats, they found themselves waist deep in wet, gritty sand, unable to move from the waist down. Panic flooded all of them and each of the friends began to cry out in fear as the Charmers floated and bobbed like feathers a short way above their heads.

~ 75 ~

Amias held up his hands and called out to his friends who were all wailing and scrambling to get free of the sodding trap they found themselves in. "Don't move! Don't any of you move! It's quicksand! If you move, you'll only sink faster!"

He was just as deep in it as they were, having come to the table a moment too late to have missed sinking with them. Padma turned to him in panic. "How do we get out of this then?"

Assessing the problem as best he could as quickly as he was able to, Amias took a deep breath. "Everyone reach for someone's hand so that we're all holding on to someone else, just try not to move too much when you do it." Then he looked back at Mr. Trumbles who was standing on the edge of the quicksand pit, as he had refused to come any closer to the Charmers or the table laden with the feast.

The Charmers flurried overhead seeming to be excited and happy, and then they zipped off into the forest leaving the friends to their slow and horrid demise.

"The Charmers are gone!" Petia gasped, watching the last of them as they vanished in the distance.

Mr. Trumbles nodded and looked back at her. "Aye, miss. They are gone right away. They only want to stay around long enough to charm ye to yer death and then they disappear."

Amias was busy working on an escape plan. "I'm not going to die today, and neither are any of you. Everyone stay still, I think I've got this worked out." He had pulled off the rope he'd had slung over his chest and was swinging it carefully over his head while trying to stay still, so that he could lasso the nearest big tree.

As soon as the rope went over a thick tree limb, Mr. Trumbles scurried up the trunk of the tree, blending right into it so that they could barely see him, and he secured it snuggly around the limb.

"Clever lad! It's tied, now come back!" the hobgoblin called out to him.

Amias held fast to the rope and then passed it to Carmo, who passed it to Petia, and from there each of the friends took hold of the rope; one to the next until they were all holding tightly to it as they sunk further down into the wet boggy sand.

Amias gripped the rope and putting one hand over the other, he worked his way up the taut line until he was hovering over solid ground near Mr. Trumbles, and then he let go of the rope and turned to help Carmo, who was struggling to pull himself out. Amias dragged the line in as fast as he could, and one by one his friends each made it to solid ground, most of them turning to help the others until each of them was safe again.

Mr. Trumbles gave them an irritated glare. "Next time I warn ye about something, heed my words! Ye could easily have died, and that's just what those evil charmers wanted."

Carmo cried out then and looked around himself in a panic. "No! Oh no!"

"What is it?" Hanne asked in concern.

His eyes shot up to her and then around to the rest of his friends. "The food! I was carrying the food! It's all gone! It was lost in the quicksand!" His voice was rigid with tension as realization nearly paralyzed him.

Every one of them looked around then and discovered that nearly everything they had been carrying had been lost in the sandy bog. Their food was gone and so were many of their things along with it.

Evren hit his knees and threw his head backward in agony. "We're going to die! We're never going to make it! Just look at us! Look at me! I'm in tatters; my best clothes are just ruined, and now most of our things are gone including all of our food! We're going to die! We'll starve!"

Amias shook his head and reached around his waist, closing his fingers over his own bag, which was cinched up tight and still full. "We won't starve. I have all my traps and fishing line. We still have enough to get by, we'll just have to be really careful about moderation."

"What about everything we've lost?" Evren shot back angrily.

"Ye aren't going to get it back, so ye do without it." Mr. Trumbles stated flatly, and he began to walk on.

Amias sighed and reached his hand to Evren to help him up. "We'll be okay. Listen, I can hunt and fish and we can eat what the forest gives us to eat. We can make tea from mint leaves and stew from red root. It's simple, but it will work. Come on now. Think of the Wish Weaver and keep your spirits up. Let's go."

"I'm going to wish that she makes me richer than the king and more beautiful than any other mortal in the world after all of this. I can't believe I'm going through all of this." Evren grumbled as he rose to his feet with Amias' help. "You're right. We need to get to her soon, so let's go. I'm tired of the trouble we keep getting into and I want this done with."

He followed Mr. Trumbles and the friends trudged along behind him, losing much of their excitement as they went. Hanne helped Petia as she did her best to overcome her pain and make her way, and Amias took up the end of the line as they all continued on their journey up the mountain.

Late that afternoon as they journeyed along in silence, they passed a pretty glen and Petia slowed her pace to a standstill, gazing into the small area covered in vines and flowers. She walked slowly into it with eyes wide and a smile filled with wonder.

Hanne stopped and turned to look at her and didn't hesitate before going into the glen after her sister as the rest of the friends also stopped to look back at them.

"What are you doing Petia?" Hanne asked with some irritation.

Petia was breathless with happiness. "Look Hanne! It's so lovely!"

Hanne looked around and shrugged. "I guess so, it's just flowers and vines, and a grassy glen. There's nothing really special about it."

Petia stared at her with a grin. "Oh, but there is! Don't you know where we are? Don't you see what this is?"

"I don't. What is it?" Hanne asked with more forced patience than curiosity.

"It's a fairy glen! It has to be! It looks just like I always imagined that it would! So beautiful." She turned in a slow circle and took in everything that she could see around her. "Look!" Her finger shot out as she pointed at the far end of the little glen. She hurried toward the area as fast as she could without hurting herself further.

The little girl came to a stop before a circle of tall graceful looking mushrooms. "Look! Oh gosh! It's a fairy ring! Isn't it incredible!" She gushed, her eyes moving over every mushroom before she turned and beamed at her sister.

Hanne frowned as the rest of their friends caught up to them and stood beside them, gazing down at the mushroom circle.

"There's no such thing as a fairy ring. Those are just mushrooms!" Hanne sighed, losing what little patience she had left.

Amias rested his hands on his hips as he tilted his head to one side and examined the circle before them. "I've heard of fairy rings, but I've never seen one before. I guess I didn't think they were real."

Petia had no interest in discussing it, she was far to enraptured with it to waste time on thoughts and words or speculation. She carefully raised her feet one at a time and stepped into the mushroom circle, grinning with pure delight as she walked slowly to the center of it.

"Petia, I don't think we should bother this. Let's just leave it alone and go. Besides, we want to get to a good place to camp for the night." Hanne frowned.

Carmo looked around the glen optimistically. "I like this spot. I think we could camp here."

Hanne shot him a dark look, but Carmo seemed confident about liking the place.

Amias bit at his lower lip and gently stepped over the mushrooms and into the circle, going to Petia and standing beside her as she turned and looked all around at it from the center.

"I haven't ever seen anything like this before." He said quietly, with clear curiosity.

Just then Evren cried out and they turned to look at him. His hands were waving swiftly through the air as he swatted at small glowing white lights near him. "Watch out! Charmers!"

Hanne noticed some around her as well, and she began to swat them away. "All of you be careful!" She added to Evren's worried warning.

Mr. Trumbles was standing nearer to Evren and he reached up quickly and grabbed hold of the boy's hand, keeping it locked in his grip. "Don't ye wave them away! Them is fairies!"

Each of the friends gasped as they stared at the little hobgoblin. "Fairies!" a few of them chorused together in amazement. Mr. Trumbles nodded.

"That's right. They're fairies, and ye be good as ye can be to them!" he scolded them all.

Padma smiled and held her hand out in the air. One soft white light landed on her and it felt like a warm tickle. Another one came, and then a few more, and she raised her other hand and let them come, as did the other children. Soon each of them had a few softly glowing white lights resting on them or floating around them, and they were all smiling and laughing quietly in wonder.

The lights began to trail away, circling a little around the children's hands before flying off in a line.

Petia was breathless. "They want us to follow them, don't they!" She exclaimed, ready to go with the little fairies anywhere.

"Aye, lass. They do indeed." Mr. Trumbles might have been hiding a smile beneath his beard and moustache, though no one could really tell for certain.

Evren furrowed his brow. "Should we go? We can't have another disaster like we had with the Charmers!" Suspicion filled his voice and knit his brow.

Mr. Trumbles eyed the boy with some mirth. "If I was ye, I'd be going with these little ones. It's quite lucky we came upon them. They're rare and they're good. Don't know about ye, but I'm going with them if they want me to."

With that he turned and hobbled away after the fairies. Amias turned to Petia and bent over slightly. "Get up on my back and I'll carry you! Let's go!"

Hanne helped her sister onto Amias' back, and they hurried after Mr. Trumbles as the others followed him, laughing and jumping, making their way in a parade of delight through the golden afternoon sunbeams.

They trailed through the forest a short way and came at last to the edge of a large emerald green pool of water, into which fell a wide and thick waterfall. The children all stopped, and Mr. Trumbles waited with them, watching as the fairies urged them onward.

Evren was bent slightly, hands on his knees as he caught his breath. "Well now what are we going to do?" He gasped, furrowing his brow at the small pretty lights ahead.

"Meesta Trumbows, are we going to swim?" Petia asked curiously as she looked over Amias' shoulder at the small hobgoblin.

Seeing the fairies head for the opposite side of the pool, he waited no longer, but instead took off his boots and waded into the water, swimming toward the fairies. The children all followed suit, quickly removing their shoes and coming into the water behind him. Carmo ran for it and jumped in, creating a great splash all around them and his friends shrieked and laughed with delight. Even Mr. Trumbles laughed quietly as they made their way across the surface of the shimmering jade water.

The fairies stopped just before the mist of the waterfall where it crashed into the pool, and when the children caught up they stopped short and stared.

~ 82 ~

"They want us to go with them into the waterfall!" Padma said in surprised reverence. "Should we do it?"

"We've come this far. Let's see where we're going." Carmo replied.

Amias was examining the shoreline around them. "Look at all these jagged rocks all around the waterfall. There's no way that we could have gotten here without swimming. There's no way to get over or around the rocks. I think the only way to follow them is to go through the waterfall."

Mr. Trumbles said nothing, but he did scowl up at the great crashing fall. Petia, who was still on Amias' back, leaned forward and spoke in his ear. "I want to go. Let's keep going!"

Amias said nothing, but he glanced at the others and ducked beneath the water, swimming under the surface as he went straight for the rushing, almost deafening turmoil directly ahead of him.

As he and Petia passed beneath the falls it roared into the water around them creating a storm of currents and bubbles, but the currents weren't too strong, and the bubbles tickled their skin as they roiled over the children's bodies.

Everyone trailed Amias' lead until all of them poked their heads up out of the water again, blinking and taking in the strange sight around them. Behind them the waterfall crashed into the emerald pool and light filtered through the falling water, giving the place they were in a soft daylight glow.

They were in a small pool of water in a rock walled cave that was about fifteen feet high and ten feet wide. They found that they could stand on the bed of the pool and the water only reached their chests.

Fairies seemed to glow brighter in the dimmer space and they buzzed about excitedly, urging the children and Mr. Trumbles to follow them. Hanne climbed out of the water and Padma helped her bring Petia off of Amias' back and onto the smooth rock floor of the cave.

"Where are we?" Petia asked as she looked around at the dark chunks of stone. Her voice echoed off the walls and bounced around the group as everyone pulled themselves from the water and brushed their hands over their hair and clothes. The fairies swirled around them in golden trails of light for a few moments and then hovered nearby them.

"I'm dry!" Evren cried out in astonishment. "The fairies dried me!"

"Me too!" Carmo added with a widening grin as he touched his clothes.

The fairies had dried all of them and were encouraging the children onward again. Petia hurried to go with them, but Hanne took her hand and made her slow down so she wouldn't hurt herself more than she had already. Sighing with a small smile, Petia relented, and the group walked together behind their bright new friends.

A sort of hallway of rock led off from the main cavern by the pool and waterfall. It twisted and turned a few times before it stopped altogether and ended at a stone archway which was covered lightly on the other side with flowering vines. The fairies laughed and zipped around in delight as they all worked together to hold the vines open like a curtain, and the children stepped through the archway into a small valley.

All of them gasped with astonishment at the sight before them as they stood together and took it all in. There was a meadow at their feet which rolled out from beneath them in grassy knolls, forming the floor of the valley. It was filled with trees dotted in groups here and there, as well as a crystal-clear spring pool with a little river running out of it and through the valley.

Encircling the valley were high mountain walls that reached straight upward a long way and then stopped suddenly where they plateaued back away from the valley, making the whole area seem as if it was one big, deep cup.

The children stared at the place open mouthed and the fairies pulled at them to continue onward. Slowly, the children followed along, their eyes locking on everything around them as they passed it, trying to see it all and not miss a single thing.

It looked very different than the forest outside the waterfall. It looked brighter, more colorful, and it seemed to be filled to the top rim of the valley with magic. Flowers grew almost everywhere, on stems and trees, on vines and bushes, and there were even some that floated along the surface of the spring and the river flowing from it. All the flowers were different, in more shades of color than any of the children could imagine.

Music sounded from a few directions and though it was different from each of the hidden places around them, it all blended together so that it made one song, like a symphony orchestra separated in parts and place, yet all playing the same music in perfect synchronization.

They followed along a path that was strewn with shimmering pebbles which felt soft to walk upon, almost like a cloud, and velvet moss in varying shades of gold, green, red, and orange.

The fairies took the group through two tall trees which looked almost as if they were sentries on guard; thick and strong, and once between them the children found themselves in a fairy village.

Fairies of almost every age in varying sizes from as small as a thumb to the size of a child's hand flew this way and that throughout the village. The village was comprised of small structures; nests and homes built of many different kinds of materials from the forest. Some were composed of leaves, some of twigs, vines on this one and flower petals on that one. Some had moss and others had fluffy feathers entwined into them. Each of them was a little different than the others around it. Some were hanging from branches of shrubs and bushes, others were nestled into the ground. All of them were pretty and welcoming. It was a patchwork quilt of homes and buildings all set about in one busy area.

Every fairy they saw seemed to be doing one thing or another, and all of them were doing their own things, until they took notice of the children and Mr. Trumbles. They slowed in their flurrying then, and most of them flew slowly to the small group of fairies which had led the children to the fairy kingdom.

There was some brief chatter amongst the fairies as they appeared to be discussing their visitors.

Petia smiled brightly and waved at them all, and some of the fairies waved back to her. Evren frowned and lowered his brow.

"What do you think they're talking about? Do you think that they're going to do anything to us?" he sounded suspicious that they might have unkind things on their tiny minds.

Padma shot him a narrow look. "I don't think they'd have invited us here the way that they did if they were going to do anything bad to us. I think our fairy guides are just telling them about us, that's all. Explaining why they brought us here."

Evren looked uncertain, but he kept his mouth shut and his eyes on what was going on, leaving his arms folded across his chest.

A few moments later, all the fairies formed a semicircle around the group and fluttered their wings excitedly. One of the largest fairies came forward. She was regally dressed in flowing material, light and shimmering, as if it was made up of moonlight on flower petals.

"Welcome friends!" She called out to them, and though her voice was soft and quiet, they could all hear her perfectly well.

"We are glad for your visit, and we would like to invite you to stay the night with us. Feast with us tonight, and in the morning you may continue on your journey!" She looked at them expectantly and the children blinked in surprise and looked around at one another.

"Should we stay?" Asked Hanne as Petia tugged anxiously on her arm.

"I'm staying." Mr. Trumbles announced without another thought about it.

"I think it would be lovely to stay!" Padma added with a smile.

Evren shook his head. "No! We can't stay here! We don't know anything about these fairies. What if they turn out to be just like the Charmers? What if they do something to us?" He lifted his chin stubbornly. "No. We have a long way to go and we can't waste time here. Let's go."

Amias looked around at the village and the mass of beautiful fairies waiting to hear the response of the children. He eyed Mr. Trumbles and his friends and drew in a deep breath, letting it out slowly.

"Let's think about this. It's late in the afternoon. We're going to have to find some place to camp tonight anyway. We've lost all of our food and most of our supplies thanks to the Charmers. I'd need to go hunting for a meal for us tonight and there isn't much daylight left. It might be wise to stay in a place such as this where a meal would be provided to us, and I believe that we'd be safer here." He spoke with his calm and even tone, and the girls smiled at him as Evren's obstinance wavered.

"Ye won't find a safer, sweeter place to pass a night." Mr. Trumbles told them. "Also, I'm not leaving until the morning, so if ye want yer guide, ye'd best be staying with me, and I'm staying here."

Evren heaved a great sigh and scowled. "Fine. We'll stay, but if anything happens, don't say that I didn't warn you!"

Padma turned and faced the fairy who had spoken to them. "We would be honored to stay, and grateful for your hospitality and kindness. Thank you for having us here!"

The fairies erupted with joy and applause, and not a moment later, they were all flurrying about again. The big fairy bowed her head to them.

"We shall prepare the feast. Please come with us to the banquet table." She and three other smaller fairies turned and flew slowly so that the children could keep up. They left the fairy village and went to a flat grassy area beside the spring.

There a table was set up quickly with places big enough for the travelers to sit and smaller places for the fairies to sit as well. Flowers and dainty dishes were set about, goblets made of tulip petals, plates made of seashells, and an array of softly glowing lights that seemed to glow brighter as the day swiftly faded into evening and the sky blushed with roses, peaches, and golds.

The music they could hear throughout the valley drew nearer, and groups of fairies began to take their places at the table with the children. Dragonflies that shimmered and shone zipped this way and that over the spring, their wings iridescent in the light of the moon that began to rise over the edge of the rim of the great wall surrounding the valley.

"Let the feast begin!" The fairy queen called out to everyone, and soft chimes sounded out over the water, echoing against the walls of the valley and rising to reach for the stars newly twinkling overhead.

Dozens of fairies brought food to the table, and the guests were surprised at the wide array of delicious dishes before them. Sweet delicate breads and juicy berries, chewy squares that tasted like maple, flower petal salads and creamy soup. Some of the food was strange to them; things they had never seen before, but they loved all of it.

When they were content, the fairies and dragonflies danced to the music for a while as blue flames wavered in small fires around the meadow by the spring. The children and Mr. Trumbles finally grew sleepy, and the fairies sent them to bed on soft woven mats of down and fluff and covered them with blankets made of the same. The group drifted off to sleep beneath the stars to the quieting notes floating over the silver lit lake beneath the moon.

Morning's light woke Amias, and when he stirred and stretched, he realized that he had never slept so peacefully. His last thought had been of his father as he was looking up at the stars, like it was every night, but for the first time in a long time he felt good about it, rather than feeling lonely and sad. The change surprised him, but he was glad for it, and he wondered if it had anything to do with where he had slept.

He looked around and saw that his friends were all still sleeping. Then he drew in a sharp breath as he looked further and saw that the whole fairy village was gone. Everything that had been there just the afternoon and night before was gone, and there was nothing but himself and his friends in the valley.

It was only then that he realized that the downy blanket which he had lain under when he fell asleep was gone, and in it's place was a strange cape. It was green, blending in so perfectly with the meadow he was laying on that it looked to him almost as if he was sleeping beneath the grass and earth of the meadow.

Picking it up to examine it, he discovered that it was feather-light in weight and was suppler than silk. He stood up and put it on, happy to see that it fit him perfectly, and surprised again when he saw the color of the cloak change. It blended in with everything around him, camouflaging him. When he moved to a different place the cloak blended in to the new place. Amias grinned with delight. He was already adept at getting through the forest and up and down the river without being seen much, but the cloak made him almost invisible as it matched him to his environment.

Carmo woke up as Amias was moving around and he rubbed his eyes and yawned. Blinking, he came to fully as he looked to his side and discovered several cloth bags.

"What are these?" He asked, glancing up at Amias. "And what are you wearing? I can only see your head!"

"It's a cloak, but it's a camouflage cloak. It blends into whatever I'm standing next to! I can hunt anything in this!" Amias was thrilled with it. "But what's beside you?" He stopped playing with his new cloak and tipped his head curiously at Carmo.

"I don't know. I just woke up and this was here. I have no idea what it is." Carmo answered in puzzlement.

"It's a gift." Mr. Trumbles replied with a grin that his beard couldn't hide. "Just like this cake that was left for me. The fairies are gone, but they've given all of us gifts!"

Carmo turned his head then and looked all around in astonishment. "They are gone!" He faced the bags beside him again. "Well, I suppose I had better have a look at these then."

Opening one bag after another he began to laugh with joy. "It's flour... and this one is sugar... and this one..." he frowned in confusion for a moment and then dipped a finger into it and tasted it. "This must be what the sweet bread was made of at dinner last night!" He jumped up from the ground and laughed out loud then. "It's food! It's ingredients for me to make breads and pastries for us! Oh we're saved! We're saved!"

Mr. Trumbles beamed gleefully. "If that's for pastries then we are saved!" Carmo and Amias laughed at him.

"I've got a bunch of flowers." Evren sighed and scowled in disappointment. "What would I want with a bunch of flowers?"

"Perhaps it's not at all about what ye want, but rather what ye need." Mr. Trumbles shot him a serious look.

"Oh, but they're beautiful!" Hanne smiled brightly at him.

Evren pouted. "They're not as beautiful as silk. I need silken cloth to be beautiful for the Wish Weaver, not flowers."

Petia smiled at her sister. "What did the fairies give to you?"

Hanne looked around the place where she was laying and saw nothing. "I don't see anything. Maybe they didn't leave a gift for me."

"Nonsense! We all got gifts!" Petia laughed softly. Then she looked closer at her sister. "What's that… around your neck?"

Hanne reached her hand up to her chest and neck and felt a metal chain. "It… it's a necklace!" She hadn't ever had any kind of jewelry before. Looking down at it, she held the slender golden chain up in the morning sun and let it sparkle. Dancing on it was a golden heart locket. She gently opened it and stared in surprise for a moment.

"What is it?" Petia asked interestedly.

"It's a mirror in a heart." Hanne sighed. "Maybe I can draw an image of Sevahn and put it in here." She looked over at Padma then. "What about you? What gift did the fairies leave for you?"

Padma sat up and stretched and then looked down at her body. "I think it's this… blanket." Over her form a sliver thin cloth was laid, almost sheer, light to the touch and light in color. She held the gauzy veil up and confusion knit her brow. "I wonder what it is."

Mr. Trumbles walked over to her then and touched the material gently. "It brings peaceful sleep. I suspect the fairies thought ye must need it." He gave her a kind smile and went back to his cake.

"What's all that?" Evren asked, pointing to a table laden with foods as beautiful as the feast had been the night before, though there were no fairies around to share it with.

"It's breakfast for us." Mr. Trumbles stated eagerly and finishing his cake off with a smack of his lips he headed straight for the low-lying table in the grass.

Hanne gasped then, and her friends turned to look at her. "But Petia! You didn't get anything! That's not right!"

Petia was holding a small brilliant white pebble in her hand and a shy smile formed over her face. "I think I did, but I don't think it's here." She pointed to a trail of the same kind of pebbles as the one she was holding. It led directly away from where she was sleeping and over a small hill. "Could you help me, please?" She asked her sister.

Hanne rose to her feet and helped Petia to hers. The small girl winced with pain. Padma came to take Petia's other side and together, they walked slowly along the trail, up over the hill. Amias and Carmo went with them.

The trail of white pebbles ended at the side of a pool of clear water, and the bottom of the pool was laid with the same white stones. It made the water seem as bright as the moon.

"Why does it stop here?" Carmo asked, trying to work out the puzzle in his head.

Amias studied the pool and bent down to touch the tip of his finger to its surface. A smile formed over his face. "Get in the water, Petia. Swim in it."

Petia laughed at first, thinking he wasn't serious, but then she realized he was and she nodded. Stepping one foot in gingerly, she grinned and looked back at her sister and friends. "It's not cold! It's quite nice actually!"

Taking a big breath, she waded in until she was up to her neck.

"Should I get in too?" Hanne asked, worried about her sister.

Amias shook his head. "No, I think this is special, just for her. I think this is her gift."

"Swimming? Swimming in a pool is her gift?" Carmo asked in confusion.

"It's not like any other water I've ever seen." Amias told them. "Swimming isn't the gift. Healing is."

With that he turned and looked at Petia who was having a grand time in the beautiful pool. "How are you feeling?" He called out to her. She ducked her head under the surface and then came rushing back up in a silvery spray, laughing.

"I feel better! In fact, I've never felt so good in my whole life!" She laughed once more and then swam down into it again.

Hanne grinned and covered her mouth with her hands as tears formed in her eyes. "A healing pool? She's healed?" It was barely more than a whisper.

"I believe she is." Amias grinned back at her.

Petia finally came back to the edge and got out, her cheeks pink and her eyes dancing with delight. "This is the best I've ever felt! All of my pain is gone!"

Padma stared at her. "You're dry! From head to toe, you're dry!" With a slight shake of her head she reached her fingers to Petia's ribs. "Your ribs are whole again. There's nothing wrong with them at all!"

"Nothing except that I'm ticklish!" Petia squealed with a giggle.

"These are the best gifts ever!" Carmo sighed with happiness.

"I'm hungry! Let's go eat!" Petia cried out, and she bounded away from them and up over the hill, her hair flying in ribboned trails behind her as her thin dress danced in the breeze. She was gone before they could catch up, until they were all at the breakfast table together.

When the meal was done they tucked the extra food away in their bags and stood up. The table vanished as if it had never been there. With a surprised shrug, the group of friends walked away from the valley and headed for the vine covered stone arch doorway that led to the waterfall and the emerald pool.

As they entered the cave, Carmo looked over at Amias who was practically invisible except for his head and hands. "Was it all a dream?" He wondered aloud.

"No one dreams that well." Amias smiled at him and they left the fairy valley behind them.

Chapter Six

Unraveled

They walked along in thoughtful silence for a while, until Evren broke it finally. "The world seems somehow terribly disappointing after being in such a magical place."

"I think the world is beautiful no matter if it's our world or the fairy kingdom." Petia smiled at him. He only shrugged.

"We have different ideas about what's beautiful." He replied simply.

"The only thing I don't understand is how it was so sunny and bright and warm in the fairy valley, but it's not that warm out here. In fact, it's downright cold, and it's not sunny either." Carmo frowned and peered up through the thick trees at what spots of sky he could see. The sky was grey and growing darker by the minute.

Amias looked up as well and paused in his step for a moment as he studied it. "I think it's going to rain. Maybe we should stop and find shelter."

Evren shook his head. "No. We've stopped too many times already. I want to get to the Wish Weaver. I want my wish granted and I don't want to wait. My beautiful clothes are already a mess; a little rain isn't going to hurt them at all."

The friends looked around at each other and Amias could see that they didn't want to argue with Evren or discuss it, so they continued onward.

Small droplets of water began to fall from the sky and sift through the leaves overhead to find the group of travelers. No one really noticed the sparse sprinkles of water at first, only wiping them away here and there, but the drops began to grow bigger and more frequent, and the wind became stronger.

Petia slowed her pace until finally she stopped, hugging herself and shivering in her thin dress as her wet hair plastered itself around her head and small face. Hanne paused and turned to look at her sister.

"What's wrong?" She asked, going to her in concern.

"It's so cold! I don't think I've ever been so cold!" the only warm part of her were the hot salt tears that rolled out of her eyes and down her wet cheeks. "I don't want to be here. I want to go home! Can't we just go home?"

Icy wind began to bluster around them, pushing them backward as if it was trying to sweep them back down the mountain. Amias, who was still toward the front of the group, saw the sisters standing alone and turned back to go to them.

"What is it?" He asked in concern, his eyes searching them both to find an answer.

Hanne sighed heavily. "She's cold and wet. She wants to go home." Then she turned to Petia. "We can't go home dear one, we've come much too far! We're so much closer to being there than home. We should keep going and complete our quest so that we can go home with our wishes. Chin up, little one. We're very close. We won't have to be out traveling much longer. You can do this. I'll help you do this."

~ 97 ~

Amias took his new cloak off and wrapped it around Petia. "Here, perhaps this will keep you warmer and dry."

The little girl looked up at him gratefully. "Thank you, Amias. You take good care of us."

He gave her a smile and shrugged one of his shoulders. "We take care of our friends. Your sister is taking good care of you, too."

Hanne hugged Petia and took her by the hand. "Come on. I'll walk with you."

"You're a good sister. The best." Petia beamed up at her.

Hanne laughed softly. "I think I have the best sister in you!"

The group began to journey on again, bowing their heads down as they pushed on through the wilding gales of wind and sheets of bitterly cold rain. None of them spoke, and all of them began to struggle as they made their ways, slipping on grass and mud, squinting their eyes against the rage of the storm, turning their faces from it, and holding their breath as they fought forward.

The light of day all but disappeared in the darkness of the storm, and Amias could barely see where he was going. He knew that it was long past time to find shelter. He turned to wave to the others and saw them strung out far behind him in a long, sparse and broken line.

"Let's find shelter!" He called out as loudly as he could, but his words were stolen from his mouth by the gale force wind. He raised his arms to wave at his friends, but all of them had their heads tucked down for protection.

He was just about to walk to Evren when a loud crack of thunder sounded almost immediately over their heads and lightning shot down from the black sky, striking a monstrous tree near them. It split at a sharp angle along the mighty trunk and with a deafening roar it crashed downward directly in the path of the children. All of them scattered away from it, desperate to get out from beneath its impact.

Evren saw the tree coming down right on top of him and he bolted. Running as fast as his feet could carry him, he rushed through the bushes and trees in the opposite direction of the falling giant. Branches whipped his face and body, tearing at his skin and shredding what was left of his once-fine clothes. Fear gripped his heart and drove him like a current through the rugged claws of every growing thing around him.

The windstorm and downpour ripped through the entire forest and all over the side of the mountain as if it was going to bring the mountain tumbling down. Evren didn't think about anything, he just ran; stumbling here and there, barely catching his balance and not looking at all where he was going when suddenly his foot pressed down on a large sopping wet leaf and slipped out from underneath him.

Crying out loudly, he tumbled downward and continued downward, rolling, bumping, banging, and crashing down the side of a deep ravine until his body finally hit the bottom of it where he lay limp, covered in mud, his skin ripped, bloodied, bruised, and his eyes closed to the world.

There was nothing but blackness and silence for an age. At long last there was the sound of crackling and the faint scent of smoke. Then there was a profound sensation of pain that grew stronger with every moment, in every part of his body. Evren grimaced and clenched his teeth against it, sucking in his breath.

Slowly, he opened his eyes, aware that he was laying on something hard, but not too uncomfortable. It was dim around him; very dim, but there was some light. It was coming from a round hole not too far away from him. He blinked. The hole took shape. It was the mouth of a cave. Looking around at the rock walls and ceiling, he realized that he was laying on the floor of a cave. It was warm and dry.

He became aware of a horrible roaring sound, thinking at first that it was tied to the pain in his head, but then he realized that it was the storm, blasting the mountain just outside of the cave.

Gasping for air through the pain that shackled him he tried to sit up to get a better look at his surroundings, but as he did so, a strange face appeared over him and two hands closed gently on his shoulders, pressing him carefully back to the stone floor.

The face belonged to an old man. A very old man with a bald head at his crown, but whose white hair fell from the back and sides of his head in long stringy tangles to his waist. He had a long white and grey moustache and beard which also reached his waist. He was scrawny, but strong, seeming to be made entirely of bone and tough muscle over it, with not an ounce of fat on his form.

His face was lined with time, darkened by the sun and worn by elements and experience. His eyes were dark as well, though they had a kindness in them that even Evren could see. The old man was quiet and still, gazing at the boy.

"Where am I?" Evren asked worriedly as panic began to flush through him. "Who are you? Where are my friends?"

The old man just watched him for a long moment and then left him, going to a small but warm fire near the mouth of the cave. Evren turned his head and was able to see most of his surroundings.

He was on a thin mat of woven reeds near the back of the small cave. Toward the front of the cave was a makeshift table built of a slab of stone resting on other stones. It sat barely a foot off the floor. Not far from the table was the fire where the old man was hovering. He was minding a pot that was hanging low over the fire.

Evren saw the man scoop something from the pot into a bowl in his hand. The man rose and returned to Evren. Helping the boy to sit up, he handed the bowl to him. It was made of wood, roughly carved, and inside it was a stew with leaves and roots in it. It smelled badly, but the old man sat near the boy and waited silently, urging him to eat it.

Evren sniffed suspiciously at it, but hunger gnawed at him and his body was cold. The hot stew would help. He closed his eyes and tipped his head back as he brought the wooden bowl to his mouth. It tasted much better than it smelled, and he had it down in no time. When he handed the empty bowl back to the hermit, the old man hurried to get more, and Evren sighed miserably.

When the hermit returned, Evren drank half the soup in the bowl and then held the warmed wood in his palms as he peered at his host. "Who are you? Where am I? Where are my friends?" He repeated his unanswered questions. The old man only sat back on his haunches and gazed impassively at the boy.

"Do you speak?" Evren asked, wondering if the old man could communicate at all.

The hermit only watched him. Evren thought perhaps he might be deaf. He scowled and tipped the bowl back, emptying its contents into his mouth and then handed the empty bowl back to the man, covering the top of it with his hand to tell the old man that he wanted no more food.

With his hunger sated, Evren looked down at his body and clothes and saw that he had been badly wounded with many scrapes and cuts, but that all of them had been bandaged. He ran his fingers over the bandages and looked up at the old man.

"Did you do this?" He asked suspiciously. The hermit only watched him in silence.

Evren pressed his lips together into a thin line, realizing that he was not going to have more than a one-sided conversation with the old man. He looked back down at his shredded clothes.

"Look at this! Look at my clothes! They're ruined! It's cold and I have nothing to wear! I have nothing to wear when I meet the Wish Weaver! How am I ever going to go to her looking this way!" He wailed and wept. The old man watched him for a long moment, and then stood up.

Taking off the soft tunic that wrapped around his whole body and fell to just below his knees, the old man handed it to Evren with wide and hopeful eyes.

Evren closed his hand around the material and furrowed his brow as irritation flashed through him. "What am I supposed to do with this? You want me to wear this old rag? You want me to wear your cast-off clothes? I can't go to the Wish Weaver in this... this... I don't even know what kind of material this is! It's trash!" He tossed it on the floor of the cave and turned his head away from the hermit.

The old man, dressed then in a short thin tunic he had been wearing beneath the warmer one, only regarded him sorrowfully for a while and then turned and went to the far wall near the fire. The hermit laid down on the stone floor of the cave and rested his head on his arm.

Evren wondered who the old man was and what he might do to Evren if he was foolish enough to fall asleep around him, but his weariness and pain overtook him, and he finally rested his head on the mat beneath him. Not long into the night he woke shivering in the cold air and he opened his eyes. The fire was nearly out, and the old man was curled into a ball, sleeping as he had been on the bare stone floor of the cave.

Scowling in misery, Evren's eyes fell on the heap of material near him. With a sigh, he reached for the tunic and gingerly pulled it on, doing his best to wrap it around himself. In moments he was warm, and he laid his head back down on the soft mat and closed his eyes, falling asleep again while doing his best to ignore the pain all over his body and find some rest.

The sound of birdsong woke him, and he opened his eyes to find that it was morning. Warm sunlight poured in through the opening of the cave, and the old man was again hovering over the fire. He stirred the contents of the pot and poured some into a bowl as he had the night before.

The hermit brought the bowl to Evren and Evren took it in silence, knowing that nothing he said to the man would be answered. It was the same kind of soup that he had eaten the night before, and it smelled as bad and yet tasted as good. He emptied the bowl and gave it back to the old man.

Evren watched as the old man put the bowl on the stone table and bent to pick up a long wooden staff which had lain on the floor behind the humble table. Then the hermit went to Evren with his tall walking staff and he reached out a hand to him.

At first the boy was sure that he wouldn't be able to get up, but then he realized that he didn't hurt as much as he had before, and that he was feeling much better.

Surprised at his improved state, he took the old man's hand, moved his legs and got to his feet with the help of the hermit. With curiosity in his eyes, he spoke.

"Where are we going?"

The old man turned and walked to the mouth of the cave, only glancing over his shoulder once to make sure that Evren was right behind him before he walked out.

Evren grumbled. "Of course you won't speak to me." He adjusted the tunic around himself and heaved a great sigh, following the old man outside.

The mountain looked as if it had been ravaged; branches and leaves were strewn everywhere, trees were broken, and some had fallen. Bushes were destroyed, and the remnants of the forest torn asunder lay across the ground as far as Evren could see.

Shock hit him like a wall, and his mouth fell open as he stared at all the devastation. He couldn't begin to guess where his friends might be or if they were even still alive.

Evren and the hermit were standing at the edge of a great precipice. There was a rock shelf at their feet in front of the cave, and the shelf was little more than a meter deep before it dropped straight down into a canyon of flora and fauna. Evren gasped when he realized that the deep ravine below them was the very one that he had fallen into, and that must have been how the hermit had found him. He wondered how the old man had gotten him from the floor of the ravine up to the cave, and he knew that since the hermit would not speak to him, he was probably never going to know.

The old man began to walk along the ridge and Evren followed him. It began to angle steeply downward, winding and twisting as they went, until it came at last to the forest floor, and Evren felt his heart quicken. He looked at everything around them, searching for his friends and calling out.

Together the boy and the old man walked; the old man silent but searching and Evren calling each of his friends by name, hoping to find that they had survived the storm.

The hermit turned suddenly and held his hand to the boy's shoulder, startling him into silence. Tipping his head slightly, the old man craned his ear away from them and Evren frowned.

"I didn't hear anything." He said in annoyance. He couldn't very well find his friends if the old man hushed him.

The hermit only looked at him so seriously that he closed his mouth. As faint as a whisper, Evren thought he heard something. His heart began to pound. He heard it again. It was a voice, calling out.

"Hello! Anyone! This is Evren! Where are you?" He cried as loudly as he could, his eyes scanning everything he could see.

He heard the voice again; it was closer. Female. He continued to call out and listen, and the hermit let his shoulder go and took off at a brisk walk toward the voice, nearly leaving Evren behind. The boy hurried to catch up, and just as he did he heard the call again and realized that it was Padma.

~ 105 ~

"Padma! It's Evren! Where are you?" He yelled out to her, and moments later she clamored out from behind a big tree.

Rushing to him, she wrapped him in a strong embrace as tears began to run down her cheeks. "You're alive! Thank goodness you're alive!"

He laughed and cried at the same time, hugging her in return. Relief flooded through him and when they finally parted, he let her go and looked at her. She appeared to have come through the storm much better than he had. She had no injuries, and only the look of someone who was tired and weather worn.

Padma gave him a good look then and moaned in worry when she saw all his bandages. "You're hurt! Oh no! What happened to you? Are you all right?"

Evren let out a long breath and nodded. "I'm hurt but I'm healing. When that bolt of lightning hit the tree and the tree fell, I ran. I remember falling into a ravine, but I don't remember anything after that. I woke up in a cave with this old hermit..." He turned then to face the old man, but the old man was gone.

"Where did he go?" Evren asked wondrously.

Padma knit her brow. "I saw him for a moment when I came around the tree, but then I was focused on you. I didn't notice that he left. Where has he gone off to?"

"I don't know. Perhaps back to the cave." Evren frowned curiously.

She eyed him better then. "Did he give you this tunic? It's nice. He must have bandaged you up and taken care of you."

With a reluctant sigh, Evren nodded. "He did take care of me." He turned his head around then. "Where are the others? Are they nearby? Are they coming to find me?"

Padma shook her head slowly. "I haven't seen them. When the tree fell, I ran too so that it wouldn't hit me. I think we all did. I haven't seen anyone since then, and I've been looking for everyone. I'm so glad I found you, though. Now we can go find the others. I hope they're all safe."

* * *

Amias opened his eyes and arched his stiffened back. He blinked in surprise for a moment as he looked around, but it was only a second before he remembered what had happened the night before.

He was sitting curled up in the hollow of a large tree. After searching in vain for his friends the night before, he had found refuge there from the storm and decided to wait it out. He knew that if he was injured in the storm while looking for his friends, he would be no help to them at all and he might not even be able to look for them, so he huddled into the hollow of the huge tree and fell asleep hoping that the storm would pass as quickly as it had come.

It was a relief to him that the morning had brought sunshine. It felt as if hope had come with it, and he desperately needed that as he climbed out of the tree and took in the sight of the disaster all around him. He had never seen such a mess, but he had also never seen such a strong storm.

None of his friends were in sight. He called out to them and heard nothing back. Worry seized his heart, but he held on to the hope that they were all safe. After looking around a wide vicinity of the tree where he had spent the night and finding nothing, he decided that rather than fanning out and trying to find all of them, he might draw them all to him, and he was sure that the best way to do that would be to build a fire.

It took some time to find dry wood and kindling, but he managed, and the sunshine and warm air helped. After a while he had a good-sized fire going, and he stood near it, his hands on his hips as he gazed at the smoke rising high into the sky, hoping that it would be a beacon to his friends.

He built a small fire and began to cook a soup, knowing that if they did find him, they would probably be hungry. He was hungry himself, and the soup helped him to feel better. When he had eaten, he went back to work gathering firewood. He determined that he would keep the bonfire blazing until they had all returned to him.

* * *

Hanne watched Petia as the small girl slept in her sister's arms. When they were separated from their friends in the storm, they had managed to find some large boulders; one of which had a rocky outcropping and they were able to squeeze in together beneath it, out of the catastrophic wind and rain. Petia had been wearing Amias' cloak, so they wrapped it around themselves to keep warm during the long, cold night.

Both of them were terrified, but Hanne was brave and held Petia all night, finding a little peace herself as she tried to comfort her sister. They had both finally fallen asleep as the storm began to clear away and the winds died down. With the morning light, Hanne felt encouraged, and she hoped that her friends would be all right and that they'd be able to find each other.

Petia stirred and opened her eyes, looking around in confusion for a long moment as she tried to remember where she was. When it came to her, she gasped and looked up at Hanne.

"Are we okay?" She worried with wide eyes.

"I think so. I'm not hurt, are you?" Hanne searched her sister's face.

The little girl shook her head. "No, I'm not hurt. I am scared though, and I'm hungry."

"I'm hungry too. Let's go out and see if we can find anyone." Hanne let go of Petia and crawled out from the hole where they'd been, and her sister followed her.

"At least the storm is gone. That's something good." Petia smiled a little as she looked around and pushed her hair out of her eyes. "Where do you think everyone is?"

Hanne sighed as she stared at all of the devastation around them. "I have no idea. I know that we're all trying to go up the mountain though, so maybe if we start walking uphill and calling out to them, we'll find them."

Petia took Hanne's hand in hers. "I think that's a wonderful idea. Maybe we can find berries or something along the way!"

Together the sisters went slowly up the side of the mountain, climbing over fallen trees, hedging around piles of debris, and all the while calling out loudly to their friends.

They hadn't been going too long when Hanne stopped and lifted her nose in the air. "I smell… something. Can you smell that?" She looked over at Petia, and her younger sister imitated her, sniffing the air as well.

"I do smell it. It's food! I smell a fire too! Someone is cooking! Let's go find them, maybe it's our friends!" She called out, and Hanne echoed her, their voices mingling here and there as they floated through the forest and up the hill.

They continued to travel toward the smell, shouting the names of their friends, and they stopped in surprise and relief when they heard a voice answer them in return.

Hanne squeezed Petia's hand. "It's Amias! We're saved!" She and Petia called out as loud as they could to him, and a few minutes later they saw Amias coming toward them at a jog.

"Girls! Are you all right? Did you make it through the storm okay?" He asked worriedly as he eyed them both for injuries.

"We made it. We stayed the night under some big rocks." Petia answered with a grin as she wrapped her arms around his waist and gave Amias a hug. He hugged them both and breath gushed out of him with relief.

"I'm so glad to hear that. I stayed in a tree last night. Come, I have soup cooking. I'm sure you must be hungry." He turned to lead them to his camp.

"Are the others with you?" Hanne asked hopefully.

He shook his head. "They're not. When I didn't see them with you, I knew that you hadn't found them either. I've built a great bonfire as a signal for them. I'm hoping that they will either smell it or see it and come to it. We can't continue on the journey until we're all together again. I'm worried that everyone is all right."

"Let's hope for the best." Hanne reassured him. "They're probably okay. They're probably all just lost, but we'll find each other again. The fire was a smart idea. It helped us to find you. It will help them, too."

Amias nodded to her and gave her a small smile. His stomach was in knots over the loss of his friends, and he was tense with worry over what might have happened to them. He got the girls fed, and continued to build the bonfire ever bigger, tending it carefully and hoping that it would be enough to reunite them all.

* * *

Evren and Padma had been wandering for a while and calling out for their friends, but to no avail. They had seen and heard no sign of them. Evren's mood was worsening as they continued on their way.

"We're never going to find them. Who knows where they've gone to or if they're even still alive." He stopped and put his hands on his hips. "Look at this! We're walking aimlessly around the side of a mountain! There's no telling where they might be! How are we ever going to find them and get going to the Wish Weaver?"

Padma sighed. She was tired of hearing him complain. "We keep looking until we find them."

Evren brightened slightly for a moment. "Maybe we just go to the Wish Weaver ourselves, and you can wish for us to find them. What about that?"

She furrowed her brow at him. "I'm not wasting my one wish trying to find our friends when we could do that ourselves. Would you want to waste your wish on that?"

He scowled and shook his head. "I can't! I have to use mine to become beautiful and wealthy! I only have one chance at this, and that's the most important wish that any of us are going to ask for!" His voice was plaintive, and his shoulders slumped.

Padma lifted her chin stubbornly. "Well then, we're not going to the Wish Weaver without them. We find them and we all go together like we should. We're not leaving anyone behind."

"Well then how are we going to find them? Because walking around aimlessly and calling out for them just isn't working!" Evren stopped where he was and crossed his arms over his chest.

Padma stopped as well and touched her fingers to her mouth thoughtfully. Brightening, she lowered her hand and pointed to a tall tree near them that had low lying branches.

"We'll climb that tree and see if we can find any sign of them from up high." She smiled at her clever idea.

Evren frowned. "You mean *you'll* climb it. I'm not going up a tree again. Climbing trees destroyed my silk clothes, and now look at me. I'm wearing this ridiculous tunic. The last thing I need is to destroy this material going up another tree and coming down a shamble. Then what would the Wish Weaver think of me? Twice ruined? No thank you. If you want to climb up that tree and have a look around, you go right ahead and do it. As for me, I'm staying right here on the ground and not dirtying myself. You might give a little thought to your own appearance too, Padma. You want the Wish Weaver to be impressed with you." He spoke as if he was dropping a pearl of wisdom in her hand.

She only rolled her eyes and sighed. "Fine. If you won't go up, I will. I'm determined to find our friends. I found you, and I didn't stop looking until I did. Now we're going to find them. I'm not giving up on any of you."

"Suit yourself. Listen, I'm grateful that you looked for me and found me. You're a good friend, but I'm not going up a tree and getting dirty."

Padma was done listening to Evren. She found the lowest branch and began climbing up it, going from one to another as she moved higher and higher up the tree trunk, until she was nearly thirty feet up off the ground.

With a grin on her face and hope in her heart, she called down to Evren. "I can see so far up here! I can see everything!" She squinted her eyes and searched over the canvas of the top of the forest, hoping with everything in her that she would make some kind of helpful discovery.

It was then that she saw a thick plume of smoke rising from the treetops not too far off in the distance. Her breath caught in her throat and she wondered if it might be their friends. She thought that it could hardly be anyone else with a campfire as far up the side of the mountain as they were. They were nearly to the top of it.

Taking careful note of the direction of the smoke from where they were, she scrambled down the tree limbs until she was on the ground again, out of breath but very excited.

Evren lifted a brow curiously. "Well, did you find them?" He asked, unwilling to believe that she could have found anything from the top of a tree.

"I might have. I'm not sure. There's a big fire not too far from here, and I hope that it's them. It makes sense that it might be them. Come on. We're going to go find out!" With that she took off at as swift a pace as Evren's healing injuries would allow, anxious to see if it was indeed her friends who were at the site of the great fire.

It wasn't long before the scent of the smoke grew stronger and the two of them could hear voices. Calling out the names of their friends with hope in their hearts, both Padma and Evren were tremendously relieved when Amias came into view, calling back to them.

"Padma! Evren!" Amias rushed to them and gave them both an embrace. "I'm so glad to see you! Are you all right?"

Padma nodded but then looked over at Evren. "I'm just fine, but Evren was hurt some. I only found him this morning."

"I was taken in by an old hermit." Evren explained, giving the tunic he was wearing a nasty look. "He dressed my wounds but then he put me in this wretched thing. I have no idea how I'm ever going to approach the Wish Weaver looking this way."

Amias lowered a brow at his friend. "You're alive and well enough, my friend. That's the most important thing. Let's get back to the others." He turned then and led them to the camp.

Hanne, Petia, and Padma all embraced one another, grateful that they were back together again. Evren went straight for the soup, talking with his friends as he did so to tell them about his harrowing adventure.

Padma looked around and frowned worriedly. "Where is Carmo? Where is Mr. Trumbles?"

Petia grew sad. "They are lost. Meesta Trumbows and Carmo haven't been here yet."

Padma's eyes grew wide. "What can we do?" She asked Amias.

Hanne walked over just then and dumped an armload of firewood on the bonfire to keep it going strong. "Well, we've got the fire. That's what brought you two back to us. We're hoping that it's enough to bring back the others."

Amias' face grew pensive. He drummed his fingers on a small stick that he had been about to throw into the bonfire as he began to pace. "Maybe we can do more. We have to be able to do more to find them than just hoping that they see the smoke and find us."

The others watched him as his mind whirred with possibilities. "We can figure this out." He said quietly, walking from one end of the camp to the other and looping around again, looking at the forest as he walked, his eyes roving over everything as if he was searching. His gaze stopped on the thin vines that hung down from the tree limbs and he stopped in his tracks.

"I've got it." He declared, turning to look at Hanne and Padma. "Climb the trees here with me and let's cut down as much length of vine as we can. We need them to be as long as we can get them. Hurry!"

Without questioning what their friend might need the vines for, Hanne and Padma both began to climb up into the trees, as did Amias, and the three of them cut down as many of the longest vines as they could.

Once the vines were on the ground, Amias put them into piles according to length. "All right. These shorter ones must be tied to the ends of the longer ones, quickly." Padma and Hanne both got to work, and Petia and Evren chipped in to help.

A short while later, the vine ropes were made. Evren dropped the last one as he finished working on it and he looked at Amias. "What are the vines for?"

Amias picked up a shorter vine and tied it around one of the big tree trunks beside him until he had encircled it fully and secured it. "All of you, tie the end of a vine rope around your waist and then tie the other end of the rope to this one I've just put around this tree. It's a leash, really. We'll all be tethered to the same tree, and we'll all have a rope around our waists so that we can venture out in different directions away from the camp, and then we'll all be able to look for Carmo and Mr. Trumbles without getting lost ourselves. We each loop our length of vine rope over our shoulders and take a direction and walk outward until we're out of rope. Then we wind the rope back up as we come back to the camp. If we haven't found them, we change direction and go back out again. Think of it like a clock. We all start at the center. We all go out and look and come back to the same place until we've gotten the whole area around us searched. With any luck, we'll find them and we won't get lost doing it. If one of us doesn't come back, the others can trace the vine rope to find us."

Padma grinned. "Amias, that's brilliant!" She bent then and tied the end of a rope to her waist. When it was knotted, she secured the other end of it to the vine rope around the tree trunk. "I'm ready." She announced determinedly.

"We're ready too. I'm going to take Petia with me." Hanne announced with her rope around her waist and Petia's hand in hers.

"I'm ready as well." Evren added. "Let's go find them."

Amias looked even more worried than he had been. "Listen, it's dangerous out there. Please, be careful. We must all make it back safely. We can't risk losing anyone or getting hurt. If you do get hurt, stay where you are and one of us will come and get you." The strain of feeling responsibility for his friends was weighing on him heavily and it was beginning to show in his expression and his voice. His friends did not miss seeing it or hearing it.

Each of the friends left the camp and headed out into the forest, careful to lay the vine rope behind them as they walked so that they could find their way back to the camp again.

For a little while they could hear each other's voices, but those sounds faded away as did the smell of the smoke from the great fire, until each of them was alone in the forest again, save for Hanne and Petia who had gone together.

Amias searched and called out loudly for his friends, but there was no answer. After a long while he sighed in resignation and walked back to the camp, carefully winding his vine up on his shoulder as he went until he got back to the tree that they were all tied to. The others who had gone out on the search had returned.

"None of you found anything?" He asked, stress narrowing his eyes and lining his forehead.

"No, there was nothing." Hanne answered as the others shook their heads.

Amias sighed deeply in frustration. "Then we go out again in different directions. We go out and we keep going out until we find them!" He threw more wood on the great bonfire as the others left, giving him sorrowful looks, then he headed out on his own again calling out as loud as he could for his lost friends.

Hanne and Petia weren't as fast as the others as they walked through the forest, but they were thorough. It was Petia, walking along behind Hanne, who stopped suddenly and gasped. Hanne turned around and looked over her shoulder.

"What is it?" She asked worriedly.

Petia hurried to the base of a tree where a group of enormous leaves was growing. "Look!" She cried out, pointing to a shoe poking out beneath one of the leaves.

Hanne followed her and helped her lift the thick, heavy leaf. There beneath it was a small boy, curled into a ball with his eyes shut. He was sweating, shivering, and moaning softly.

"Carmo!" Hanne gasped. She reached her hand out to him to shake him awake. He would not open his eyes. "Carmo, it's Hanne and Petia, wake up! Please, wake up!"

The boy did not awaken. Hanne touched his face with her fingertips.

"He has a fever. He's very sick." Rising to her feet, she began to quickly untie the rope from her waist.

"Hanne! What are you doing? We'll be lost!" Petia panicked as she watched Hanne hurrying with the vine.

"No, we won't be lost. Listen, I'm going to tie the rope around you. You stay here with Carmo. We can't get him back by ourselves. He's too weak to walk. He'll have to be carried. I'm going to follow our rope back to the camp to get the others and I'll be back. I want you to stay here with him and watch over him. We'll follow your rope back here so that we can find you again. Just don't leave him and don't take the rope off, and I'll be back with the others. You can do this. Be brave." Hanne tied the rope around Petia's waist.

Petia looked up at her sister. "I'll be brave like you. Hurry and get them! I'll stay here with Carmo."

Hanne sighed and kissed Petia on the cheek before heading back into the forest as quickly as she could, tracing the vine back to the camp. When she arrived, all of the others were there again.

"Amias! Padma! Evren! We found him! We found Carmo!" Hanne cried out to them as she ran into the camp, doubled over breathlessly.

~ 118 ~

"Where is he, and where is Petia?" Padma asked in concern as she looked behind Hanne.

"Why aren't you wearing your rope?" Amias demanded, giving her a sharp look.

Hanne caught her breath as well as she could and stood straight again. "I tied my rope around Petia and I left her with Carmo. She's there to stay with him and watch over him until we can get back to them. I followed the rope back here."

"Why didn't Carmo come back with you?" Evren asked, walking toward Hanne with widening eyes.

"He's sick. He's very sick. He wouldn't even wake up when I tried to rouse him. He's got a fever, too. I can't carry him back. I need your help to get him back here." She looked around at her friends and saw the worry she felt take shape on their faces.

"We'll make a hammock out of the cloak that the fairies gave me. We can tie it to a solid branch and carry him back in that." Amias plucked his cloak up from the place he'd set it on the ground along with a few of his other things.

Padma picked up a long, thick branch from their pile of firewood on the ground and together they all hurried along Petia's vine rope until they got to the end of it. There they found Petia trying her best to take care of Carmo, who still had not awaken. It was as if he was in a daze and could neither see them nor hear them, though he wasn't fully asleep.

Working quickly, Padma and Amias tied the ends of his cloak to the pole she'd brought, creating a hammock with it. With gentle hands, Evren, Amias, Hanne, and Padma lifted Carmo and laid him in the cloth, wrapping it carefully around him. Petia began to wind the vine rope up on her shoulder as she led the way back along the vine to the camp as the others followed her; Hanne right behind her, then Evren and Amias carrying the pole from which Carmo hung, and Padma at the rear.

When they reached the camp, Hanne and Petia made a thick bed of leaves for Carmo and Amias got to work gathering ingredients from the forest around the camp. In a short time he had what he needed to make a stew of roots, leaves, and flowers. The others hovered close in case there was anything that he might need for them to do.

"That smells wretched!" Evren choked when he leaned over to sniff the finished stew.

"It might smell awful, but it will do Carmo some good." Amias told him as he sat beside Carmo on the ground. Padma knelt down and rested Carmo's head on her lap, leaning him up a bit so that Amias could feed him. Carmo didn't resist the stew, though it was difficult for them to get it down his throat at first. He still wouldn't wake fully, but they did get him to swallow most of the brew before they laid him back down to rest.

Padma laid her gift from the fairies over him; her cloth of peaceful dreams, and she tucked it around him closely. "Maybe this will at least ease his mind while his body heals." She said quietly.

"That was thoughtful. I'm sure that it will help." Amias gave her a small smile.

Evren sat at Carmo's side and stayed there, watching over his friend. Hanne and Petia gathered more ingredients for the smelly stew Amias had made, knowing that Carmo would probably need more of it.

Amias went off from the campsite a short way and leaned his back against a tree stump as the stress and strain of their journey finally overwhelmed him. Emotion rushed through him and he began to shake and cry, sinking to the ground as the weight of it all consumed him.

"Amias?" Padma's soft voice sounded through his sobs. He looked up to see her coming to him. She knelt quietly beside him and wrapped her arms around him to hug him for a long while. Not feeling the strength to hold anything in any longer, he rested his head on her shoulder and cried until he had no more tears. She let go of him then and he drew in a big breath and leaned his head back against the tree behind him, looking up at the late afternoon sky beyond the canopy of the forest.

"I don't know how I ever thought that I could look out for you all. I can't believe I was so certain that I would be able to get you all through the forest to the Wish Weaver safely. This is far too much responsibility! It's incredible that we're all together again, except we're still missing Mr. Trumbles. We've been chased by wolves, almost killed by Charmers, we suffered through a storm and we all got lost. Petia and Evren got hurt, Carmo is so sick that I don't even know if he'll make it, and we aren't even there yet! We don't even know where we're going! How did we ever think that we could make it on this journey? Our families must be so worried! At least your family. My uncle probably has no idea that I'm gone." He closed his eyes and groaned before turning his head to look at Petia. "This is just too much responsibility for me. I shouldn't have come. None of us should have come."

She listened to him and gave him a gentle smile. "Amias, the responsibility isn't all on you. It's on each one of us. We've made it this far because we've relied on each other. It's true that most of the time we've been

~ 121 ~

relying on you, but that's because you know the forest so well, and you were much better prepared for this journey than all of us. We're lucky to have you with us, but you aren't here as a guardian. You're here as a friend; an equal. We all have a responsibility to look out for each other and that's what we have to do. That's what we are doing."

He sighed then and wiped the drying tears from his eyes and face. "I know you're right. I feel like I must look out for all of you. Maybe I'm trying to be the father that I don't have."

Padma smiled at him and held her hand out to him. He took it and she helped him to his feet. "All you have to be is our friend. We all take care of each other."

Amias sighed with relief then. "I know you're right. Thank you." He gave her a hug and they turned and went back to the camp. Hanne and Petia were laying the ingredients that they had found beside the small fire where the stew was cooking.

"We got more roots and leaves for you!" Petia told him with hope in her eyes.

He patted her shoulder. "Good. Carmo is going to need them." He made more stew and spent a long while that night helping his friends to feed it to Carmo. Late in the evening, with the bonfire still burning bright in hopes of bringing Mr. Trumbles back to them, they all fell asleep.

When Amias woke the next morning, his first thoughts were of Carmo. He went to the bed they had made for him and found Carmo awake. Padma was with him and she smiled at Amias.

"His fever is down. He's doing much better." She looked much more at ease than she had been the night before, and it gave Amias some relief to see it.

"I'm so glad to hear that." He sat beside Carmo and his younger friend looked up at him.

"I am feeling better. Padma gave me more of the soup you made for me. Thank you all for taking such good care of me." His voice was weak and his eyes were half closed, but there was more color in his cheeks and he was more himself than he had been.

"That's good Carmo. Keep eating the soup. Those herbs and roots will help you get better. You need to rest more. We're going to stay in this camp another night so you can heal. All those wishes can wait one more day." Amias gave Carmo a pat on the arm and turned to look up at the others who had gathered around them.

"I think you're right." Padma nodded. "We can stay one more night."

"Our wishes will wait." Hanne agreed.

Amias sighed. "The wishes will wait and perhaps Mr. Trumbles will come back to us and help us get to the Wish Weaver. It would be much easier to find her with his help, and I want to know that he's all right too."

Chapter Seven

The Wish Weaver

Feeling more confident with Carmo on the mend, Amias took his fishing line to a river nearby the camp with the intention of catching breakfast for them all to eat. They still had food from the fairies, but he knew that he could add fish to the stew and it would be better for Carmo.

The river wasn't too wide; there were fallen trees over it in places which connected both banks, but it was plenty deep, and Amias knew there would be big fish in it. He was right, and he had already caught five large river fish when he thought he saw something moving through the bushes on the other side of the river, opposite him.

Amias rose slowly and quietly from the rock he had been sitting on, his eyes locked on the leaves he had seen wavering across the water. A moment later his heart skipped a beat as he realized that he was watching one big leaf move through other leaves, and he thought that he might know just what it was. It looked like a big leaf hat. One that belonged to a friend of his.

"Mr. Trumbles?" He called out, knowing he would probably scare the fish away and not caring too much about it. "Mr. Trumbles, is that you?" He raised his voice a bit more. The moving leaf stopped and a moment later a small old face popped out of the leaves and looked straight at him.

"There ye are me boy!" the hobgoblin brightened, giving him wave of his hand. The little man disappeared into the leaves again and Amias went from feeling elated to feeling panic flood through him again as he tried in vain to see where his small friend had gone to. A moment later he saw Mr. Trumbles race nimbly over one of the fallen logs that spanned the width of the river, putting him on Amias' side of the water, and two moments after that, the hobgoblin was at Amias' side, beaming up at him.

"I wasn't sure what had happened to ye!" Mr. Trumbles was almost giddy with joy at having found Amias, and Amias felt the same.

"I wasn't sure what happened to all of us! Everyone got lost in the storm." Amias told him with a huge sigh.

"Aye, it was a terrible storm. The worst I've ever seen!" Mr. Trumbles knit his brow in concern and then sat on a nearby stump, placing his hands on his knees and looking up at Amias. "Has everyone been found?"

"Yes, Mr. Trumbles, you were the last of our company who was lost. I'm so glad that you're here and that you're all right." Amias felt a wave of relief wash over him, leaving him with some semblance of peace in its place.

"Is everyone all right?" Mr. Trumbles asked with concern in his eyes.

Amias shook his head slowly. "Not really. Evren was hurt, but he's healing, and Carmo was very sick. I made a root and herb stew for him and he's getting better, but he's still quite ill."

Mr. Trumbles leapt off the stump where he'd been sitting. "Take me to him right away."

Pulling his catch of fish out of the shallow water at the bank, Amias slung them over his shoulder. "Let's go." He replied, and they went straight back to the camp.

"Meesta Trumbows!" Petia called out happily when she saw the hobgoblin. "You're back!"

"It's so good to see you Mr. Trumbles!" Padma and Hanne both grinned at their small friend.

"It is good; now we can find our way to the Wish Weaver." Evren looked pleased.

Mr. Trumbles gave the children a nod, but he went directly to Carmo and began to look the boy over closely. "It's good that we came when we did, Amias." He said quietly. In the blink of an eye the hobgoblin left Carmo's side and began to zip through the forest around the camp in a near blur. He came back just a few minutes later and took one of Amias' cups from beside the fire, pouring some water into it. Amias went to him and watched as Mr. Trumbles opened his hand. In his palm were dark purple flower petals. He crushed the flower petals between his hands, rolling his fingers back and forth over them before dropping them into the hot water in the cup. As he slowly stirred the flower petal tea he was brewing, he looked over at the stew and sniffed at it.

"That's a good stew for him. Clever of ye to use those roots and herbs, Amias, but this will set the boy right again." With that, Mr. Trumbles took the cup to Carmo and sat him up, giving it to him to drink. "Here, drink it all. All of it. Don't mind any if those petals go down too. Ye need them."

Carmo did as he was told to do, and when the tea was gone, Mr. Trumbles took the cup back. "Lay ye down now and rest. Ye need that too." Carmo laid his head back down and a few moments later, he was sleeping again.

As Carmo slept, his friends sat around the fire, finally able to talk and relax some since they were all back together again. They shared stories of their experiences in the storm, and the group told Mr. Trumbles how they had found Carmo and brought him back to the camp. He praised them some for their cleverness and teamwork. He told them what they knew in their hearts; they never would have made it as far as they had without each other.

Amias stared up at the night sky that evening, taking in the vastness of it and thinking to himself that perhaps his father was somewhere beneath the same stars that he was looking at. He hoped that his father was safe, and that he would see him again sometime soon. He thought about the journey that he and his friends had experienced, and he was grateful that they were all together again.

It was a long while before his mind let him fall asleep, and when he did his dreams were filled with the same hopes he had in his heart.

Morning brought with it sunshine and cheer, as the group of friends woke to find that Carmo was much better. He was so much better in fact that he was up baking for them all and creating a delicious breakfast before any of them had opened their eyes.

Padma and Petia laughed and hugged him, glad to see that he was himself again. Mr. Trumbles went to him with a big smile and eyed the baked treats that Carmo was making with the fairy ingredients he'd been gifted with.

"Those look tasty!" He said, reaching for one.

Carmo smiled wide at him. "I thought you'd like those. I made them to thank you for helping to heal me. To thank all of you. I know I wouldn't be here right now if it wasn't for each of you coming to find me, bringing me back here to camp, and working to heal me. I'm grateful."

"You're a friend. We take care of our friends." Amias said with a kind look as he took a pastry.

They all ate together and then packed up the camp, ready for the road while the morning was still young.

"Let's go! We have wishes to make!" Evren urged them as he picked up his step a bit. He'd had some of the dark purple flower tea that Mr. Trumbles had made for Carmo, and he was feeling much better too. He was more than ready to get to the Wish Weaver.

"Has your wish changed?" Petia asked him as they headed through the trees and up the mountain again.

He shook his head. "No. I'm going to wish to be beautiful and wealthy. If I'm beautiful and wealthy, then everything will be perfect in my life. I won't want anything else."

"I don't want wealth. I just want Sevahn to love me. I want to matter to him. What's a person even worth if they're not loved by another?" Hanne sighed with a sad sort of expression and Petia took her hand.

"I love you. You mean everything to me." The little girl beamed up at her. Hanne smiled back at her.

"I love you, too. I meant a different kind of love." Hanne shrugged, and they continued to walk. Amias gave both Evren and Hanne a sorrowful look, wishing they could see themselves as he saw them.

"Well my wish is the same." Padma added, and then she looked over at Amias. "Are you going to wish for anything?"

"No." He shook his head.

~ 128 ~

"I thought that you might have changed your mind since you came along on the journey, and since we'll be there anyway." She eyed him with kindness.

"There's nothing I need that I don't already have." He replied simply. "I only came along to look after all of you."

Petia grinned at the hobgoblin. "What about you, Meesta Trumbows? Are you going to wish for anything?"

The small being gave his head a resolute shake. "Definitely not."

All the friends were a little surprised at his resolve, but no one asked him about it.

They journeyed on through the day and that evening they reached the edge of a great lake which stretched out before them, ringed with towering trees all around, and one rugged mountain peak, which was the tip top of the mountain just off to one side. The peak was shorter than the lake was wide.

"Are we here? Did we make it?" Evren asked anxiously as he grew breathless at the idea.

"Aye lad. We're close. The Wish Weaver is just across Stargazer Lake, on the other side." He motioned the furthest point over the water with his finger.

Carmo frowned. "How are we going to get over there?"

"Ye will have to find a way to get there. Ye canno' go around it; there is no way." He pointed then to the towering trees and the children realized that just behind the trees was a cliff wall that went straight down, save for the place where they had come up and the mountain peak on the left side of them.

"Well there must be some way across. People get there and come back. The traveler who came through our

~ 129 ~

village, Nassim, he was coming here. I'm sure he made it too. He's not sitting on the bank here, so there must be some way." Padma was standing near the water with her hands on her hips, assessing the situation.

Amias studied the area around them. "The bamboo." He said quietly, nodding toward a spot just a short distance from their group.

Padma frowned slightly. "What about the bamboo?"

Amias began walking toward it. "There's a grove of bamboo trees right there. We can cut down several stalks of it and tie them together to make a raft." Taking his small hatchet out, he began to hack down towering stalks of it, and all the others helped him to pull them down. When there were enough of them gathered, Amias bound them all together until they formed one big flat raft.

By that time, Carmo and Hanne had an evening meal readied for them, and they made camp for the night, excited and nervous about the following day and what they would find. Most of them stayed awake much longer than usual; their thoughts swirling with possibility and hope.

They woke up late the next morning, partly because they had stayed up so long the night before and partly because there was very little sunlight to rouse them. Fog had enveloped them and shrouded almost everything but the camp; nothing beyond that was visible.

After they had eaten breakfast, they worked fast to break their camp down and get themselves packed up and ready for the journey across the lake. Amias made certain that everyone was onboard his raft safely, and then he gave them paddles he had made of bamboo stalk tied to wide, flat pieces of tree bark. He explained to them how to row together so that they could move forward faster

~ 130 ~

and not go in circles or go nowhere at all. After a few practices, they all had it down and they were ready to go.

With Stargazer Lake shrouded in mist and fog, they made their way slowly and carefully in a hushed silence. The only sound around them was the splashing ripple of water as the oars moved through it. Nothing more could be heard, and the children kept quiet for a long while.

Evren was the first to break the silence, but even he barely spoke above a whisper as he did so. "Are we even going anywhere? I can't see anything in this fog and it feels like we've been going for hours! How do we know we've gotten anywhere? For all we know, we might still be on the shore we left, and we haven't gone an inch!"

Mr. Trumbles turned to look at him as he kept rowing. "We're moving. Don't lose heart, lad. We're definitely moving."

Evren scowled and continued to row, though it was clear that he wasn't happy about it. Amias peered into the mist as far as he could and saw nothing. "I know we set off in the right direction when we left the shore. I think we're still going the right way. I just wish that this fog would lift so that we could see our way toward the other side and the Wish Weaver."

As the last word left his lips, the fog before them began to part, not much wider than their raft, leaving the surface of the water visible and the way ahead clear. The parting fog had formed a narrow canyon around them, though there was still fog above them. It was almost a tunnel through the mist, and at the farthest end of it they could just barely see a shoreline.

"That's... that's incredible! Did you see that?" Padma asked her friends as they all stared at the same thing. "How is that even possible? I don't understand."

"I guess we have a way to the Wish Weaver now."
Evren spoke with an even tone. He wasn't sure if he was
happy about it or not. Something about the way that the
fog had parted when Amias spoke made him uneasy, as it
did the rest of his friends.

They paddled on in silence again, staying within the
fog canyon walls, which seemed to be held in place,
though the fog above them and to the sides of them
swirled mysteriously, the canyon they were in never
changed.

When they were near enough to see the shore clearly,
Carmo gasped. "What's wrong with the raft?"

"What do you mean what's wrong with it?" Evren
asked, looking around worriedly.

"I'm not rowing, and we're still moving." He
answered, and his friends each pulled their oars out of the
water slowly, realizing that he was right. Their raft was
gliding across the glassy surface of the lake without a
single one of them guiding it with an oar. It was as if the
boat was being pulled by some gravitational force.

Without further discussion, each of them laid their
oars beside them on the raft, staring at the water and the
shore ahead, wondering what strange thing might be
happening to them. Even Mr. Trumbles kept silent.

The raft did not waver from its path through the fog
canyon, and it did not stop until it reached the shoreline
where it came up far enough onto the shore that the
children were able to walk off of it without getting their
feet wet.

"How did that happen?" Petia asked quietly,
squeezing her sister's hand and looking up at her with
wide eyes.

"I don't know." Hanne answered honestly, wondering the same thing herself.

"Well, I guess we must be here. So where is this Wish Weaver?" Evren asked, looking at the thick forest around them.

Amias dragged the raft up onto the shore further and tied it to a tree, wondering if it might leave without them if he didn't. With that done, he turned and looked at the forest. At first, there was nothing he could see around them but trees and bushes; growth all over in every direction. Then the shape of something in the grey afternoon light caught his eyes.

"There... that's not a tree. What is that?" He asked, walking toward it. His friends followed him, picking their way carefully through the flora and fauna. The thing he had his eyes on became clearer and he blinked in surprise.

"It's ruins... it's... it's ancient ruins. It looks like it must have been a castle or stronghold a very long time ago." He continued toward it and the others trailed in line behind him, all of them looking at everything they could.

The closer he got to it, the surer of it he was. "It is ruins. I think this must certainly have been a castle many years ago. See how it looks as if there were different rooms here? I know it's nothing but short, broken walls now and everything is covered in moss, but you can see how it used to have some sort of shape." He pointed along the edges of the remains and the others could imagine what he was showing them to be walls that connected and made rooms in what must have been a great structure at one time.

"I don't like this place. Something about it doesn't feel right." Petia spoke in a plaintive voice as she held tightly to Hanne's hand and eyed everything around her.

"It's just old. There's nothing to be afraid of." Evren dismissed her fears.

"I think she's right. I don't like it either. This place is old, but that's not all. It's enchanted. Something happened here." Mr. Trumbles bristled and glared about suspiciously.

The children grew quiet again as they tip-toed through the ruins, going from one skeleton of a room to another.

"Where is she?" Evren whispered impatiently.

Amias stopped suddenly and Evren crashed into the back of him and lost his breath for a moment. "Shh. Look. I think that's her." He was standing at the edge of an archway, and he pressed close against it to hide himself. Pointing subtly, he aimed his fingertip through the arch and his friends all leaned carefully around his shoulder, arm, and waist as they crowded together to peek.

Through the archway was a set of broken stone steps that led down into a lower expanse of ground about four feet deeper than where the children stood. It was a big area that had given way to nature long before.

Looking through curtains of vines draped thickly from gnarled old trees and twisted limbs at the far end of the area, they saw her. In the moss and ivy-covered crumbling remains of what might have been a conservatory at one time, sat an old woman. Her hair was long and wavy, shimmering white and silver as bright as the moon.

She rested on the edge of what was left of a great pillar that had broken and collapsed, leaving once-grandly-carved chunks of columns strewn about the place where she was. Before her there was a fire which she stared into with downcast eyes, holding a teacup in her hand as she

~ 134 ~

gazed at the flames. Beside her was a spinning wheel and a strange looking loom.

The old woman was wrapped in a beautiful tapestry cloak, vibrant in color and design, which fell from her shoulders all around her and trailed on the ground long past her feet. It was filled with bold and deep reds, warm oranges, bright yellows, every color of green and shade of blue, luxurious purples and earthy toned browns. It was the most beautiful cloak any of them had ever seen.

"That's her! That has to be her!" Evren gushed in a whisper. "What do we do now?"

"I'm staying here. I don't want anything to do with her." Amias stated flatly.

"I'm saying as well." Mr. Trumbles added. "You won't see me down there with her."

"I'm going to go down to see her." Padma said quietly as she stared at the woman.

"I think we should all go down together." Hanne suggested, looking at her friends. "Those of us who want to make wishes. Amias and Mr. Trumbles don't have to go, they can stay here while the rest of us go down and get our wishes granted, and then we'll be right back up here and we can all go home."

Evren's brow lifted hopefully. "That sounds easy enough."

"Hanne, I don't want to go, I'm scared." Petia bit at her lower lip as she lifted her eyes to her big sister.

Hanne gave her hand a squeeze. "Well that's okay, you can stay here with Amias if it's all right with him."

Amias nodded. "Of course, that's fine."

Petia shook her head rapidly. "No, I want to be with you! I just don't want to go down there to see her!"

Hanne sighed heavily. "Petia, we've come all this way. I came so that I could see her and get a wish. You only have two choices right now. You can stay with Amias or you can come with me, but I'm going."

Petia's hand trembled in her sister's grasp. "I'll come with you." She whispered.

Padma reached for Petia's other hand to encourage her and she looked at her friends. "Well, shall we go?"

Carmo, Evren, and Hanne nodded. Amias' shoulders dropped as he let out all of his breath and watched them head cautiously down the stone steps. "Good luck." He whispered to them.

Mr. Trumbles furrowed his grey brows and began to pace with his hands behind his back. Amias stood behind the stone arch and peered around it at his friends and the Wish Weaver who was sitting at the fire.

When the friends got close to the fire, the old woman looked up at them, and they all stopped in their tracks. Amias' heart nearly dropped from his chest as he saw her eyes. They were bluish and silvery, and they glowed softly, as if there was blue firelight in them. He had never seen eyes like that on anything. Stifling a gasp, he leaned forward just a bit more and tried to listen as well as he could from his hiding place.

"Good evening." She greeted them. Her voice sounded as mysterious as the fog just behind them on the lake; not frightening, but old, soft, and strange. Amias blinked and looked around. It was evening. The afternoon had vanished somehow in the mist, and the grey light of day had given way to a very dark night. He turned his attention back to the Wish Weaver and his friends. He was surprised that while they were a fair distance from him, he could still hear what they were all saying just as if they were near to him.

"Good evening." Padma spoke as they others huddled close to her. She cleared her throat. "We've come seeking the Wish Weaver."

The old woman smiled and her softly glowing eyes moved over all of them as if she was regarding them closely. "You've found her. Please, sit and join me." She lifted her knobbly old hand and indicated the chunks of broken columns around the fire, here and there. The friends turned and looked at them with uncertainty, and after a long moment of hesitation, they each sat on one.

"I am called Kayda." She told them as she stood from her seat on the great base of the broken pillar.

Evren drew in a deep breath as his heart raced in his chest. "We've all come with a wish." He told her earnestly. He knew that he was moments from being all that he had dreamed of being.

She nodded to him. "Of course you have. We have time. We have lots of time. Please, join me in having some tea. We must observe pleasantries first, mustn't we? It isn't often enough that I get visitors. I'm sure you've come a long way. Certainly, hot tea would be refreshing." She bent near the fire and her hand moved over a stone there. A tray appeared with five cups on it, all filled with dark tea.

Kayda walked to Evren and held the tray out to him. He wanted his wish to be granted right then and there, but he realized that he couldn't be rude and refuse the tea if he was going to ask her to make him beautiful and wealthy. He took a cup and gave her a nod of thanks.

She went next to Padma and then to Carmo, followed by Hanne and at last, Petia. Each of them took their cups of tea and watched her as she sat back down once more. She held her own cup aloft to them. "To wishes being granted." She toasted them. They nodded and all of them drank their tea.

"Finish it all. We must be polite." She advised them. They did as she bid them, and Evren beamed.

"It's so good! Buttery and warm. It's the best tea I've ever had!" He emptied his cup and looked over at his friends, glad that he'd had it.

"It is good!" Padma added, and Carmo and Hanne agreed with her. Hanne looked over at her sister to ask if she liked it, but Petia was sleeping on the column. Hanne smiled wistfully at her. "Poor girl. She's so tired. We've come quite a long way."

Just then Padma yawned and smiled. "I know how she feels, I'm tired too."

"Do you think it would be all right if we…" Evren tried to say, but he nodded off and slumped over on his column.

"I think it would be fine for just a few…" Padma answered him, but she fell asleep before she could finish saying it. Hanne yawned then and though she tried to keep her eyes open and on the Wish Weaver who was gazing silently at her, she too nodded and sleep overtook her.

Amias gripped the stone archway. "They're sleeping! All of them!" He whispered to Mr. Trumbles. "What's happening?"

His heart racing in his chest with worry for his friends, he took a step forward toward the stairs and stepped on a twig. It snapped beneath the weight of his body, and the sound echoed through the forested ruins like a shot. The Wish Weaver's softly glowing eyes flashed, and she stared straight at him.

Sucking his breath in, he spun back to the shadow of the archway and prayed silently that he hadn't been seen. Mr. Trumbles, who was hiding on the other side of the back of the archway lifted his hand to his mouth to shush Amias. He shook his head and held a finger over his lips. Amias nodded slowly and frowned. He hadn't meant to step on the twig and he desperately hoped that he hadn't given them away.

Kayda rose from the pillar base where she sat, and she walked slowly toward Evren, reaching her hand out to touch him. As she did he woke, rubbing his eyes and looking up at her.

"Oh! I must have fallen asleep. I didn't realize. What were you saying?" He asked, trying to focus his mind on whatever it was that she might have been saying when he had dozed off. He didn't bother to look at his other friends, he was too enraptured with the Wish Weaver standing before him. He stared into her eyes and knew that his wishes were about to come true.

"I wonder if you might tell me about your tunic." She asked, her eyes locked on him. "Where did you get it?"

Evren blinked and looked down at the tunic the hermit had given him, and his stomach clenched as his heart fell. "Oh no! I knew I should have dressed better. When we left the village, I didn't know how long it would take to get to you, and I wore my best clothes. I wore silk so that you would see how good I look in silk, and how I should be dressed in it every day. You would see how I need it so desperately. We got into a few spots of trouble along the way though, and my beautiful silks were torn and shredded! We were separated in the storm and I was lost. Some ratty old hermit found me and took me to a cave. He must have stolen my silk clothes, or what was left of them, and he put this on me. I'm so sorry, I really was dressed better for you. I meant to impress you, I did, but that horrible old man put me in this and now I look awful!" He felt as if his whole future might just crash right around him.

"What do you think of this gift that the hermit gave to you?" Kayda asked, her eyes burning into the depths of him.

Evren's shoulders drooped and his eyes lowered to the ground. "It's truly wretched. I only continued to wear it because it's kept me warm and dry."

Anger flashed in Kayda's eyes, but Evren didn't see it. "What is the wish that you will ask of me?"

Drawing in a deep breath, he squared his shoulders and lifted his chin. "I wish for great wealth and tremendous beauty."

She seemed to stare right through him. "And what do you think great wealth and beauty are?"

He blinked, expecting that she should know the answer to her question. "Well, it's more money than I can ever spend, and I want to be the most handsome man in the country."

Kayda's eyes narrowed. "Come with me."

She turned away from him and Evren rose from the stone column piece and followed her. She took him to the spinning wheel and sat down at it. His heart raced in his chest as he realized that he was about to be granted his wish. She was going to weave it into reality for him.

Her feet began to move the pedals and she spoke as she sat there, looking off into the distance, never turning her head to look at him. "Put your hand on the spindle."

Evren did as she bade him, wrapping his hand around the spindle and holding tightly to it. The wheel began to spin, first slowly and then it spun faster and faster. He began to feel dizzy watching it, and everything around him began to spin. For a moment he thought he might fall over, but then another sensation overtook him. He felt as if he was being stretched and pulled, spun and twisted. Pain wracked his body and he tried to cry out, but sound was ripped from his mouth. He tried to pull his hand from the spindle, but he could not feel it any longer, his body began to feel stiff and he discovered that he could move no part of it. All he could see was a sea of colors and nothing else. He cried out, but there was no answer. There was nothing but silence.

Kayda stood before Padma and reached her hand out to touch her. Padma gasped and opened her eyes suddenly, looking around as she jolted awake. "What… what happened? Did I fall asleep? I'm so sorry. I didn't mean to."

"You're awake now. What is the wish that you would ask of me?" Kayda studied the young girl's green eyes closely.

Padma's breath grew short as she looked up into the Wish Weaver's face. "I… I experienced a tragedy when I was a child. I wish that it had never happened."

Kayda was silent for a long moment and Padma began to wonder if she had wished for too much, but then Kayda nodded. "Come with me." She led Padma to a nearby tree stump. It was a wide circle with more rings in it than Padma could guess at. She knew that it must have been an extremely old tree when it was cut down.

The Wish Weaver reached her hand out and touched the tip of her finger to the center of the rings. Padma stared in wonder as the rings in the wood began to ripple as if they were water, and the whole circle before her turned silver as the ripples moved outward from the center of the stump.

"Look down into this." Kayda instructed her. She did as she was told, barely believing that she was looking down into a tree stump. A scene unfolded before her, as if it was real life happening right in front of her eyes. There was a river going through a forest, and beside the river she saw a woman washing clothes against some large rocks. She heard the cry of a child and the woman looked to see a small boy who had been playing not far from her. He fell into the river with a great splash and though he thrashed with all his might, in no time at all he was sucked under the surface of the water by the current of the river. Padma felt as if she was right there on the riverbank watching it all happen in person and she cried out, feeling an urge to run and help the boy, but realizing that she was frozen in place.

The woman who had been washing clothes dove in after the boy and Padma watched helplessly. The woman was a good swimmer and she went down again and again searching for the small boy until at last she came back up with him and carried him to the riverbank. Laying his still body in the grass there, she pressed hard on the boy's chest, but he didn't move. Padma was certain that the boy must have drowned. She felt as if her heart would break at the sight of it. The woman pressed again and again at the boy's chest and finally he coughed out a good amount of water and opened his eyes, blinking and looking around in utter fright. The woman scooped the boy up into her arms and held him close for a long while before letting him go.

Padma realized that the boy was going to be all right. Sighing in relief, she turned her head and looked at

Kayda, feeling strange to be back in a dark forest when she had just been certain that she was standing at the side of a river in the bright morning sunlight.

"Why... why did you show this to me?" She asked in utter confusion.

The Wish Weaver tilted her head slightly. "Look again... look closer."

Padma did look closer and the boy became her single focus. She saw that he was wearing a necklace with a wolf claw hanging at the end of it. Turning her head once more away from the sunny day on the river, she looked back at the Wish Weaver standing beside her in the dark night.

"A wolf claw necklace? I don't understand. I know only one person who wears a wolf claw necklace, and that's Omid. Omid saved me from the wolf when I was a child. It is to him that I owe a debt that cannot be repaid." She frowned, wondering what the old woman was getting at. "Is this the future or the past? Is it real? Who is the child? What have I seen?"

"You may only know what you have already seen. Do you still intend to ask for your wish?" Kayda studied her intently.

"Yes." Padma stated resolutely. "Yes, I still want my wish, please. I wish that I had never gone into the forest that night and that Omid never had to save me."

Kayda's face was impassive. "Very well, come with me."

She went to the spinning wheel and sat, instructing Padma to put her hand on the spindle. Padma obeyed. Kayda began to spin the wheel. Around and around it began to whirl, faster and faster yet as Padma grew dizzy and felt as if her whole being was coming apart. Her body trembled with pain and she tried to let go of the spindle, but everything around her spun and she was lost in color. When the spinning stopped, she felt as if she was frozen in place. She called out and tried to struggle, but there was nothing that she could do.

Amias had finally caught his breath and he looked over at Mr. Trumbles, who was watching him intently. Moving slowly and silently, he leaned around the edge of the archway and looked down to the fire where the Wish Weaver had been sitting with his friends. Frowning in confusion, he saw that Evren and Padma were gone. He looked around, wondering if they had gotten their wishes and were on their way back to him, but he couldn't see them anywhere.

Mr. Trumbles also peeked around the corner and knit his brow, returning to the shadow and looking at Amias. "Where are they?" He barely whispered. Amias shrugged and shook his head. As slowly and silently has he had a moment before, he slipped his face around the edge of the mossy old stone and looked down on the scene again, wondering what he had missed and what was going on.

Kayda was standing over Carmo as he slept. She watched him for a little while, and Amias watched her. She finally reached her hand out and touched it to his cheek. He opened his eyes sleepily and pushed himself up to a sitting position with a yawn. Looking around, he saw that only Hanne and Petia were still there with him, and they were both sleeping.

Jerking his face up to look at Kayda, his voice filled with panic. "Where are my friends?"

She tipped her head to the side slightly. "They've gotten their wishes." She answered him quietly.

"They have? Is it time for me now? May I have my wish please?" He asked with wide eyes and a growing smile. Hope filled his heart.

Kayda watched him steadily. "And what is it that you wish for?"

Carmo folded his hands together and spoke in a reverent tone. "My grandmother is very sick, and the doctor says that she won't be with us much longer, that her time has come to pass on. I can't stand the thought of losing her. My wish is that I can keep her with me all of my life, alive and healthy. I want more time with her. A lot more time."

Kayda's glowing eyes narrowed slightly. "And what does your grandmother want?"

The boy frowned slightly and looked away from her for a moment. "I... I don't know. She said that she wanted to spend all her remaining time with me, but I know if I got my wish, she could have the rest of my life with me."

The Wish Weaver's eyes flashed, and she set her mouth in a thin line. "Come with me." She said coldly. She went to her spinning wheel and sat down, working the pedals as she stared straight ahead. "Hold on to the spindle."

Carmo reached his hand up and closed his fingers around the wooden piece. Everything began to spin around him and he grew dizzy and breathless.

"What... what's happening?" He pleaded. "Is this my wish? Why is this happening?"

Kayda spoke as her feet moved the pedals swiftly. "This is happening because you had a selfish wish, because you only thought of your own desires and not once of what your grandmother wanted for herself!"

Like the others, Carmo was whirred into pain and color and then stillness. He cried out as well, but like the others there was no answer.

Amias stared in horror, frozen to the spot as he saw what was happening below him. He could not begin to wrap his mind around it, no matter how he tried. There was no understanding it, and beyond that there was no believing it.

Kayda roused Hanne. Hanne opened her eyes and rose from the column, looking around her. Petia was still asleep beside her. Before Hanne could speak, Kayda answered her coming question.

"Your friends have gotten their wishes. Now it is your turn."

Hanne moved to wake Petia and the Wish Weaver stopped her. "No, do not wake her. She is weary as you said. Let her sleep. This time shall only be for the two of us. Tell me, what is it that you've come to me for? What is your wish?"

Mustering up her courage, Hanne cleared her throat and somehow found her voice. "I want to wish for love. For real love." She twisted her fingers nervously. "You see, there's a boy in my village whom I love with all my heart, and I want him to love me in return. He only has eyes for Padma, but she doesn't like him that way. I desperately want him to love me. I want to be his."

Kayda pursed her lips in thought. "And who are you without him?"

Hanne didn't even have to think about her answer. She knew it in her heart of hearts. "Nothing… I'm nothing at all without him. He is my whole world."

The Wish Weaver sighed and turned to the spinning wheel. "Come with me."

Hanne's heart thudded against her chest as happiness sprung up in her. Sevahn was finally going to love her forever, and she would be his and he would be hers. Kayda turned to look straight at her.

"Put your hand on the spindle."

Hanne did as she was told to do. Kayda sat down and began to spin the wheel. Around and around it went, and the faster it went the dizzier Hanne became and she felt as though she was coming apart at the seams of her heart. Crying out in pain and confusion, she struggled against the spinning, but when it finally stopped she found that she could not move, and there was nothing but color and silence around her.

Amias was trembling with anger and fear. "We have to do something! We have to stop her!" He whispered to Mr. Trumbles. "What can we do?"

Mr. Trumbles shook his head and held his hands up. "Ye know as much as I do. I've no idea how to stop her or help them!"

Closing his eyes and searching his heart and mind, he tried to think as logically as he could. She was a weaver of wishes, he rolled the thought around in his head. A weaver, he repeated silently to himself. He thought about what he had seen and what she had done, playing the ghastly scenes of his friends with the old woman over in his mind. He had to find a way to undo what she had done. He had to find a loophole. Everything inside him stopped suddenly and his eyes flashed open.

"That's it! A loophole!" He whispered to Mr. Trumbles. The hobgoblin only frowned and shook his head in confusion.

"I have a plan." Amias gave his small friend a serious nod. "Stay here and watch over me. If I don't make it back with everyone then go to the village and tell them what's happened. Help them to get here so that they can save us."

The hobgoblin nodded. "I promise." He whispered back. "Ye are the cleverest of them. If anyone can save them, it's ye. Go on now. I'm watching ye. I'll keep me word."

Amias held his breath and gave Mr. Trumbles a nod. With his heart in his throat, he crept from behind the archway and with great care he lowered himself almost to the ground and crawled down the steps to a nearby bush, getting closer to the fire and the Wish Weaver.

Kayda stroked Petia's head with her hand and the small girl woke slowly and rubbed her eyes. When she looked up and realized that she was alone and her sister was gone, she began to weep miserably, but Kayda comforted her.

"Do not cry, your sister has made her wish. It is now your turn."

Petia only shook her head. "I don't want a turn!"

Kayda stared at her. "What do you mean? Don't you have a wish?"

Petia wiped at the tears on her cheeks. "No, I didn't come with a wish. I only came to be with my sister! Where is she?"

The Wish Weaver frowned. "She isn't here."

"I want her! If she isn't here, then I have to go back to Amias!" She turned and began to leave, but the Wish Weaver reached for her and held her arm.

"Do you want to make a wish that you could be with her?" the old woman offered.

Petia glared hard at Kayda through her tears. "No. I don't want a wish. I don't want to be here. I just want to be where Hanne is! I'm going back to the village with Amias!"

Kayda held the girl fast in her hand. "I can send you to where she is. You'll be there right away."

"I'm not going to wish it." Petia stated stubbornly.

With a sigh, the Wish Weaver eyed the little girl carefully. "If you won't make a wish, then make me a trade."

"A trade?" Petia asked, puzzled. "I don't have anything to trade."

Kayda took the girl's hand and led her to the spindle. "Oh, but you do. Trade me the last moment of your life and I'll send you to your sister. You may have all of your life but the very last moment. That will be mine. For that I will send you to your sister right now."

Petia thought about it and tried to figure out if she was being tricked. She worked it over in her mind. If it was only the last moment of her life then there wasn't much that she was going to be doing with it anyway, it was going to slip away from her and then she would pass on as her grandfather had, and that wouldn't be so bad, she thought. Only the last moment of her life in trade for being with her sister right then seemed like a good idea. She bit at her lower lip as she pondered it.

"Hurry, now." Kayda told her sternly.

"Okay." Petia mumbled. "I will make the trade."

Amias drew nearer to the space where the fire was. Kayda's voice had quieted, and he could no longer hear what she was saying. He could only glimpse that she was standing beside the spinning wheel with Petia.

"In order for this trade to work, you need only to touch the tip of your finger to this." The Wish Weaver held up a large black thorn.

Petia's eyes shot from the thorn up to Kayda's softly glowing eyes. "What is that?"

"It's a bloodthorn." The old woman answered.

"What does it do?" the little girl asked with uncertainty.

"It guarantees me the last moment of your life."

"Does it hurt?" Petia felt fear overwhelming her like a tidal wave.

"Yes, it will hurt, but you will get to be with your sister." The Wish Weaver held up the bloodthorn and Petia's fingertip hovered over the razor-sharp tip of it. Closing her eyes and gritting her teeth, she pressed her finger down. It felt to her as if fire shot through her fingertip, up her arm, and straight into her heart.

"Ouch!" She cried, opening her eyes and looking at her finger. It was red, except for one little black spot where the bloodthorn had poked her. She tried to rub it away, but the black spot began to grow a little.

"Why isn't it going away? What's happening?" She asked quietly.

"You're running out of time, little one." Kayda said evenly. "You made a choice. You could have had a wish, but you didn't want to make one, so this is the only other way that you can be with your sister. Put your hand on the spindle there."

Petia's heart hurt as if something was pinching it from the outside. She furrowed her brow wincing in pain, and then she reached up and put her fingers around the spindle.

Kayda's feet began to move the pedals fast and Petia grew dizzy as darkness wrapped itself around her. Kayda's feet moved even faster, and Petia felt herself being pulled apart.

"Hanne!" She cried out. "Hanne, where are you?" Her small body quivered with pain, and then everything stopped and there was nothing but stillness. The darkness gave way to some faint light and color, and the form of Hanne's face became clear to her though nothing else did.

"Hanne!" Petia cried out, struggling to move. "I can't move! I can't reach you!"

Hanne wept. "I can see you, but I can't move either. I'm stuck, Petia. I can't reach you, but I can see you. I can see you sister."

Amias stared, terrified as he watched Petia disappear. He had never been so afraid in all his life, but he knew that he had to do whatever it took to get to his friends, and he hoped with everything in him that his plan would work.

Chapter Eight

The Loophole

Amias waited until the Wish Weaver was sitting on her pillar again. All of his friends were gone, though he had only seen how some of them had disappeared. He suspected that all of them had gone the same way.

It was a horror unlike anything he had ever seen before. One moment they had been standing there holding on to the spindle, and the next they had become a blur of swirling light, as if their bodies had been spun into glowing colored threads, whirling around in circles where their bodies had once been, and then the thread wove itself through the loom beside the Wish Weaver, and when it had formed its piece, it lifted magically from the loom and floated down to join the tapestry of her magnificent cloak. Every one of his friends had been added to her cloak, and Amias realized then why it was so long and so colorful. It was filled with the souls of people who had come to her for wishes, and she had weaved them right into the tapestry that she wore.

He wondered if she ever truly granted a wish, or if anyone who came to her was doomed to be imprisoned. The thought passed from him. He wasn't concerned with wishes, he was solely focused on the task of finding a way to free his friends, and he knew by watching her that he had one chance and one chance only to try his plan. If it didn't work, he would be trapped as well and then there would be no hope for them unless Mr. Trumbles worked a miracle and got their families there to try to save them.

He watched her for a long while as she sat before the fire holding the cup of hot tea in her hand. She did not drink it, she only held it and stared at the flames, her bluish glowing eyes unmoving as if she was somewhere else in some other time and place.

Building up his courage, he rose from his hiding place and walked toward the fire, going to sit beside her on the far side of the fire where she was sitting, rather than the near side of the fire where all of his friends had sat with their backs to the archway where he'd remained hidden. He knew that he had to be on the far side of the fire for a couple of reasons; one of which was so that Mr. Trumbles could see his face and could see what was happening. The other reason was that if he wasn't there beside her, his plan might not work the way that he needed it to.

Turning her head slowly, she tore her eyes from the fire and looked at him. He felt as if she could see right through him, but he steadied the fear in himself and swallowed hard. "Wish Weaver?" He asked with a wavering voice. He cleared his throat. "Are you the Wish Weaver?"

The light in her eyes flared up for a moment as she gazed at him. "You know that I am. What is it that you seek?"

He shrugged. "I want only to warm myself by your fire, if I may. It is a cold night."

Kayda watched him closely. "It *is* a cold night. Perhaps some hot tea will warm you. Would you like some?"

Amias nodded. "Yes, please." He answered, and she turned her head away and walked toward the fire, leaning down to wave her hand over the flat stone there. A cup of hot tea appeared.

As she was bending over to create his tea, he slipped silently to the back of her long tapestry cloak and pulling his knife out, he cut the very edge of it. Taking one of the threads that came loose where he'd cut it, he tugged on the string until there was a short length of it, and he tied it around his ankle.

Kayda turned then and walked toward him, handing the cup of tea to him. "There are. What is your name?"

"I am Amias." He answered. "And you? What is your name?"

"You may call me Kayda." She replied and took her seat again on the base of the pillar, though her face stayed turned to him and her eyes did not leave him.

"I am from the village Zorion." He told her, hoping that he wasn't giving any part of his plan away. She seemed to be able to see more of him than he wanted her to.

"You are. You've come a long way." She watched him. "Aren't you going to drink your tea?"

He shrugged. "It's very warm. I am waiting for it to cool."

She narrowed her eyes some and he knew that she didn't believe him. "Have you come all this way only to have tea with me and sit by my fire to keep me company, or have you come with a wish?"

"I have no wish. Although, I would like to learn to weave. Would you please teach me? You must be quite a weaver if you can weave wishes into being." He forced himself to give her a smile of admiration. He hoped that she would believe it.

Surprise showed itself on her face and in her eyes, and she was quiet a moment. "No one has ever asked me to show them how to weave before." She told him, and she was still for a few beats of his heart. "I will show you. Come with me."

Together they went to the spinning wheel and the loom. Sitting him on the bench there, she took a regular string and showed him how to pull it from the wheel and then weave it through the loom, bringing the string in and out and tightening each row as he went.

When he had it fairly mastered, he turned to her and smiled. "Thank you. A learned skill is always valuable."

She studied him curiously. "Are you certain there is no wish that you could ask me for?"

Amias was thoughtful for a moment, making a small show of it by holding his finger to his chin and looking upward as if doing so might give him some idea of what to wish for. Then he looked at her.

"Some of my friends came to see you tonight, and I could wish to be with them." He suggested. "I haven't seen them, and they were to meet me back at the raft on the lake. If I was to make a wish, it could be for that."

"I can grant that wish." She smiled coolly at him. "Put your hand on the spindle."

He reached his hand up but before he closed it around the piece, he stared straight into her glowing eyes. "I know that you will weave me into the tapestry of your cloak. Before you do that, I will include this in my wish: that you will enable me to have contact with all my friends, because I am lonely for them."

Kayda's mouth twisted slightly. "Because you already know what will happen and yet you go willingly to them, I will also grant that wish. You will be trapped either way, so it makes no difference."

Amias thought that his heart might just beat itself right out of his chest, he was so afraid, but he gripped the spindle tightly and hoped against hope that his plan would work.

The Wish Weaver sat on the bench and her feet flew swiftly over the pedals. Everything around Amias began to spin and blur, and though the pain that shot through him was horrible, he gritted his teeth and closed his eyes, willing himself to get through it. He could hear the voices of his friends; all of them, crying out to him and warning him not to do it, to let go of the spindle, but he held on with all the strength in him until the spinning stopped.

When he opened his eyes again, he found himself surrounded by color. He realized that he was gently and loosely woven into the tapestry. With great effort he found that he could move painstakingly slowly through the fabric. He could also hear all of his friends, and he could see them, though they were in different places.

"Amias! I felt you coming here! I tried to tell you to stop!" Carmo called to him. "I think I'm alone here, but I felt you! I think the Wish Weaver trapped us both!"

Amias understood then that he was the only one connected to all of his friends, none of them were connected to each other, save for Hanne and Petia who were near enough to see each other and to speak, but not close enough to reach out to touch the other.

"Carmo, all of you, you are all trapped here in the Wish Weaver's tapestry and you can't see each other, but I know that you can all see me, and I know that you can hear me. I'm here because I have a plan. I'm here to save you and get you out of here!" Amias felt determination in his heart. He vowed to himself that there was no way he would fail. He couldn't. The lives of his friends were at stake.

Moving with every bit of strength that he could muster, he struggled to move through the fabric until he got to Petia. When he reached her, he pulled at the thread that he had tied around his ankle, leaving it tied to him and drawing up the other end of it.

When he had a good length of it, he tied it snugly around her wrist and knotted it, and then made his way to Hanne. When he reached her, he tried to calm her crying.

"Hanne, I believe that we're going to make it out of here. I have a plan. You must believe that it's going to work. I need you to help me. Please, don't cry. Stay strong." He spoke gently, and she listened to him.

"Okay. I'll do anything I can." She promised. He pulled more of the thread loose and tied it around her wrist tightly, so that both she and Petia had the thread tied to them in a chain.

Amias moved to Carmo and then Padma, and finally Evren, tying it to the wrist of each friend tightly until they were all together. "You're all tied now!" He told them, knowing that they could not see or hear each other. "I brought this thread from the outside of her cloak and when she wove me into the tapestry, she didn't know that she was weaving a loose end in. I couldn't be sure that if I pulled it from the outside that I could get to any of you, and I couldn't be sure that she wouldn't stop me, but I knew that if I pulled it from the inside, she wouldn't be able to stop me because we're already woven into the tapestry."

"Amias, that's brilliant!" Padma called out to him.

"I'm going to pull on this thread now and keep pulling on it! With any luck, it will undo what she's done and free us. We're all tied together so that I can't lose you. As soon as you can move, help me pull the thread!" He began to pull harder on it, winding it up like a fishing line, reeling it in, circling it at his feet, reeling it in some more, slowly and steadily, pulling as hard as he could, over and over.

He pulled on it for a long while, bringing in much more thread than he thought he would be, when finally the tapestry began to unravel at the farthest point that he could see. The sight of it coming apart built his hopes up and he began to pull harder, though it strained everything in him to do it. The unravelling grew closer and closer to him, and the closer it got, the less strain there was.

Amias could hear voices calling out joyfully as the thread drew nearer to him; many, many voices, all of them crying out with relief as they were freed, one by one. He heard a loud scream from the Wish Weaver as even more of the cloak unraveled, until he heard his friends shouting with joy that they were free. Evren first, then Padma, followed by Carmo, Hanne, and then Petia. Amias was the last to be freed, and when the final loop of thread fell at his feet, all that was left of it was the short string tied around his own ankle. He bent down and untied it and it vanished. He found himself standing with all of his friends, and many more people than that. There were hundreds of people all around him, all of them in shock and elation at having been freed from the tapestry.

It was then that Amias realized that he couldn't see Evren. "Where is Evren?" He asked worriedly as they found themselves in the very midst of chaos. People all around them were talking and shouting and running.

"I'm right here!" Evren's voice sounded, and the group of friends looked down to see a big, beautiful peacock standing beside them.

Padma frowned. "Is that you, Evren?"

"Of course it's me. Who else would it be?" He demanded sharply.

"But, Evren…" Carmo said gently, "You're a peacock. A talking… peacock."

Evren shrieked and cried out miserably, but Amias couldn't worry about Evren at that moment. He turned hastily and searched for Kayda.

"The Wish Weaver! She's got to be here!" He shouted, and then he saw her. "If we defeat her, everything will be restored. I know it. Evren, you'll be a boy again."

Kayda stood before them, her long silvery moonlight hair cascading around her, her bluish dark eyes shining brightly, and she was standing in a plain, long white robe that reached from the top of her shoulders to the ground. She was unmoving, as if she was in shock.

He raced to the spinning wheel and took the seat, clasping her hand tightly and closing it over the spindle. His feet raced over the pedals, and he expected to be weaving her into thread as they had all been, but as she began to spin and cry out, she did not become thread.

White lights formed where her body was, whirring about in the shape of what was once her form, until there was no form, there were only threads of bright light spinning, until they vanished, and in their place was a white glowing mist. The mist began to take shape, and all the friends stared in disbelief as the shape became that of a horse. When it was finally fully formed, the horse reared back, and on its head grew a long, spiraled white horn.

Amias stared as Mr. Trumbles ran to them and took Petia's hand in his. "A unicorn?" Amias spoke in a low voice filled with consternation.

The unicorn walked to Amias and bowed its head. Kayda's voice sounded clearly from it. "Amias." She said as she looked into his eyes. He saw that the same bluish firelight was in her dark black eyes. It was beyond magical.

"I have been under a curse for more than a century. I was once a princess and I lived in this beautiful palace which is now no more than ruins. I was in love and I was going to be married to a prince, but a cruel witch outraged with jealousy over the prince, cursed me and turned me into a unicorn. I tried to escape as a unicorn, but then she transformed me into an old woman; into the Wish Weaver, and imprisoned me here. I had to collect a thousand souls to free myself from the curse and become a unicorn again. I hated doing it, but there was no choice for me. She forced me to do it. Only the selfless souls could receive a wish and escape me. Anyone who wished for anything for themselves would be trapped in the tapestry. The witch fed on greed! My prince defeated the witch in battle and when he did, he became a black stallion. He was doomed to walk the earth in search of a way to free me. Her death was not enough to destroy the curse, but it did weaken it. When you came here I hadn't yet captured a thousand souls; far from it, but when you freed all the souls I'd been forced to capture and spun me out of being human, you broke the curse. I have returned to my unicorn form now. You've freed us all with your selfless act and your cleverness. Thank you." She bowed low to Amias and all his friends stared at her.

"I am grateful for what you have done. I will grant you all a safe journey home, as safe as it can be." She looked at Petia then.

"What about me?" Evren demanded, going up to the unicorn and pecking his beak at her leg. She reared up and he backed away from her. When she had all four hooves on the ground again, she eyed him and spoke with a strong voice.

"You have not returned to your former self because you have not learned your lesson. This is solely due to your own vanity. You're going to have to break this curse yourself. It's not from me, it's a residual of the evilness from the witch, and it's hung on to you. You won't be free of it until you change on the inside." She turned then and faced Amias again.

"Thank you for freeing me. You have done a great deed. You've freed all these people as well as me. There is nothing but goodness in you, Amias, and you will be greatly rewarded for it. Farewell." With that, Kayda left them, running to the edge of the lake and then right over the surface of the water, disappearing in the fog across the lake, and the fog left with her, lifting and vanishing as morning light began to shine brightly all around them.

People who had been trapped in the tapestry began to fan out, looking for ways to leave, and as the crowd thinned, a voice shouted out above the others, and the group of friends turned to face it.

"Amias! Amias!" A man cried out, rushing toward them.

His heart stopped in his chest and his mouth fell open. "Father?" He asked in disbelief as the man threw his arms around him and buried the boy in a strong embrace.

"Amias, I thought I'd never see you again!" The man wept as Amias realized just who it was that was holding him, and then he wept as well.

"Father! Father! What are you doing here? Where did you come from?" Amias finally let go of the man and looked up into his father's eyes.

"I came to the Wish Weaver after your mother passed away. I came to wish that she could be brought back. I thought that I couldn't bear to live without her, but what I learned was that I couldn't bear to live without you. My lesson was in letting her go. I was punished by the Wish Weaver for not holding on to what I have, but letting it go to try to grasp for what was gone from me. I never should have left you! I know that now. I was trying to make our family whole and in coming here I only broke it apart. Please... please find it in your heart to forgive me somehow. I beg of you." His father fell to his knees before Amias, and Amias hugged him tightly around the neck.

"I understand. I do. I forgive you, but please come home with me. Please come back home. There's nothing that I want more than that." Amias' voice was filled with emotion and hope.

"I'm coming back with you. I'm taking all of you back to the village. We're all going home." Amias' father stood up and ruffled his son's hair. "You've grown so much, and I've missed it. I've missed it, but I'll do everything I can to make up for it."

Evren was walking around on his bird legs and found the tunic that he had been wearing when he was woven into the tapestry. He plucked it up with his beak and took it to Carmo.

"Carmo! Carmo! Tie this to my back, please." Evren the peacock asked miserably. Carmo knelt to the ground and gently tied it to the bird's back.

"Are you sure? I'll carry it for you, Evren." Carmo offered sweetly.

Evren made a strange bird noise. "No, I'll carry it. It's my burden to bear."

Mr. Trumbles stood beside Amias, and the boy introduced him to the man he had not expected to find on his journey. "Mr. Trumbles, this is my father, Cruz. Father, this is Mr. Trumbles, the hobgoblin. He's been a lifesaver for us and he helped get us here."

"I'm very glad to meet you, Mr. Trumbles. Thank you for taking care of these young ones." Cruz reached down and shook the little creature's hand.

"They've taken care of me, too." Mr. Trumbles blushed red and waved his hand. "Come, we want to get back to the other side of Stargazer Lake while it's still light out."

He led the way and minutes later they were all on the raft. They saw that many other people had found their own ways across the lake and were getting away safely. Hanne sat quietly and thoughtfully as they all rowed, but a short while later she turned to her friends with an odd expression on her face.

"I feel different." She said curiously.

Amias tipped his head and looked over at her. "Different in what way?"

Hanne thought for a moment before she answered. "When I was trapped I got to thinking about what the Wish Weaver asked me about my wish, before she took me to the spinning wheel. Her questions stayed in my mind and made me reconsider my answers. When I came

~ 163 ~

here I thought that I needed his love in order to be worth anything, but now I can see that I was wrong. It doesn't matter whether Sevahn loves me or not. His love doesn't define my worth. Not at all."

With that she picked up the golden heart locket around her neck. "I think the fairies knew that I needed to learn that when they gave me this locket." She opened it up and looked at the reflection of her face in the mirror inside it. "I'm a good sister. I'm a good friend. I'm a good person. I like who I am. Actually, I love who I am without him. She asked me that… what am I without him. I told her I was nothing without him, but I was so wrong. I'm so many wonderful things without him. When I realized that while I was trapped, I also realized that I don't need him with me to be happy. I'm already happy on my own."

"You've gained some wisdom!" Cruz smiled at her. "I learned my own lessons too, being trapped by her. I had everything I needed right there before me, and if Amias hadn't come and saved us all, I might never have gotten him back. I'll never leave again."

Amias smiled at his father and Cruz rubbed his hand over his son's head, ruffling the dark waves of hair there.

They reached the other side of Stargazer Lake and made their way down the mountain. It seemed to them that going down the mountain was faster than going up, and they were surprised when they reached the place where they had camped after the storm, before sunset.

"Let's stay here. I have something I need to take care of." Evren said quietly as he scratched his peacock claws in the dirt near the dead bonfire.

"I agree. We can have a good meal and night's rest, and be off early in the morning." Amias nodded to him.

Hanne looked at Petia who slumped down onto a nearby log to rest. "Petia, are you tired from walking today?"

Petia shrugged. "I'm not feeling well." She said quietly. Hanne frowned and went to her, touching her hand to Petia's forehead.

"You look pale, but you don't have a fever. Are you hungry?" Hanne gazed at her in concern.

"No, I'm not hungry at all." Petia replied.

"But you haven't eaten anything today." Hanne sat beside her and took her sister's fingers in hers. At Hanne's touch, Petia winced and withdrew her hand.

"Ouch!" She whispered, tucking her fist in her lap.

Hanne narrowed her eyes. "I hurt you? How can that be? Show me your hand, please."

Petia held her hand up and Hanne cried out loudly. Padma, Amias, and Mr. Trumbles ran to them. Carmo, who was cooking, set his work down and hurried to them as well. Evren was gone from the camp. Cruz was out getting firewood.

"What... what is this? What's happened to your hand? To your arm?" Hanne held her sister's arm gently and stared at the horror before her.

The inside of Petia's finger had turned black, as well as her palm, and from her palm spreading all the way up the inside of her arm was a black web of lines. It went as far up as the base of her neck.

All of the friends were shocked and worried. Petia felt tears building up in her eyes. "I didn't want to bother anyone about it." She said quietly. "I thought when the Wish Weaver changed back to the unicorn, this would go away. I guess it didn't."

"How did it happen? What is it?" Hanne pleaded with her.

Petia sighed and looked down at it. "I didn't have a wish. I didn't want to make a wish. I just wanted to be with you. The Wish Weaver told me that since I wouldn't make a wish, the only way that I could get to you would be if I gave her the last moment of my life. I thought that wouldn't be so bad, so I made the trade with her. I gave her the last moment of my life and she let me go to be with you in the tapestry."

Mr. Trumbles scowled and shook his head. "This is a dark curse. This is the curse of death. It's in yer blood and it's gone through yer veins to yer heart. There's no stopping this. Ye are dying slowly, but I don't think ye will be with us much longer."

Tears fell from Petia's eyes. "Will I make it to the village?"

Mr. Trumbles shook his head. "No, I don't think so lass."

Hanne's heart almost stopped. "You... you traded your life to be with me?"

Petia used her free hand to wipe the tears from her eyes and cheeks. "Only the last moment of it. I didn't think the last moment would be so soon. I thought it would be a long time from now, when I'm old."

Mr. Trumbles raised his eyes to meet hers. "The Wish Weaver brought that moment much closer to the present. I see why she did it. There was no other way to get yer soul, and she was cursed. Made to get yer soul one way or another."

"We have to find a way to undo this! I can't lose her!" Hanne wept miserably as she wrapped her arms around her sister and held her tightly.

"There's no way to undo it. I'm sorry, wee ones." Mr. Trumbles said quietly as he took Petia's free hand in his and gave it a squeeze before turning and walking to the center of the camp.

Amias sank to his knees before them, and Padma sat on Hanne's other side, taking hold of her hand. Carmo knelt beside Amias and they wept together. When Cruz returned to the camp, Mr. Trumbles explained what they had discovered, and even Cruz had to agree that nothing could be done. He vowed to carry Petia in his arms back to the village so that she could save her strength and perhaps last longer.

Evren searched a long while for the hermit's cave, but he couldn't find it. He thought back to when he and Padma were lost before, and how she had climbed up into a tree to get a good look at the forest around them. He had scoffed at the idea when she had done it, but she had been right. He flew up to the lower limbs of a tall tree, and branch by branch he made his way up to the top of it, stunned by the fantastic view from such a lofty place. Turning his head this way and that, he searched for the cave, and at last he saw it not far off.

Evren made his way back down the tree carefully, and lit onto the ground, heading in the direction he'd seen the cave. He finally made it, walking up the long rock path along the cliff above the ravine. He thought about how he had nearly fallen to his death there, and how the hermit had saved him.

Hesitating a moment at the mouth of the cave, he drew up the courage deep in himself and walked inside. His eyes adjusted to the darkness within as he looked about. The hermit was sitting at the fire, and he raised his eyes to the peacock standing before him. He made no move, he only watched curiously.

Evren spoke, hoping he didn't surprise the hermit too much. "I… I'm changed. I was the boy who you saved during the storm. You brought me here, taking me out of the ravine and carrying me to this cave. You were so kind to me, tending to my wounds, feeding me, giving me your own bed to sleep on while you slept on the stone floor here. You gave me your own clothes to wear, and yet you have so little. You gave me everything that you have, and when you did it meant nothing to me."

The hermit only watched him, and Evren moved closer to him, walking slowly. "I went through a strange experience, and it made me think about who I am. It made me think about what true beauty is. I thought it was being handsome, but it's not. You showed me true beauty. It's the kindness in a selfless heart. The fairies tried to show me beauty in the flowers that they gave to me. Beauty is inside of us, and all around us in the world, it's not what we look like, but what we give to others and how we treat others. I saw that my own heart was empty and the beauty that I wanted was nothing but a shell. Now I want to be beautiful on the inside and you've shown me how to do that."

Evren drew near the old man and stopped beside him. The old man continued to watch him. "I wanted to be wealthy, and I thought that meant having a great deal of money; more money that I could ever spend, but your gifts; giving all that you had to me without a thought for yourself showed me what wealth is. This tunic, though simple, is worth more than any silk I might cover myself with, because it was given to me when you had so little to give. That generosity makes the gift of this tunic priceless. No material could ever compare to it. I've never worn anything so precious."

The bird tugged at the strings around the tunic with his beak and the tunic fell to the floor from his back. "I'm returning it to you. As you can see, with feathers I won't need clothes. Thank you for your kindness and compassion, and for all that you did for me. I hope that your kindness is returned to you tenfold."

"You have learned a great deal." The old hermit said to him, and Evren was shocked to hear him speak.

"I have, thanks to you and to the Wish Weaver." Evren answered. "I must go back to my friends. Thank you." The bird turned then and walked to the mouth of the cave and the hermit watched him go.

As Evren crossed the threshold of the cave, light shone bright around him as if he was at the center of the sun. He squinted and held his hands up to shield his eyes. It was then that he realized he had hands rather than wings. Blinking, he looked down and saw that he had become a boy again. With a sharp gasp, he also saw that he was wearing the tunic that he had just given to the old man. Reaching his fingers down to it, he touched the soft material and lowered his brow in confusion.

Turning in place, he looked back into the cave wondering how he was wearing the tunic when he'd just left it behind him with the hermit. There was nothing in the cave. No fire, no stone table, no soft mat bed, no wood bowl or cup, and no hermit. Everything was gone, and the cave was barren. Evren cried out for the old man and went back into the cave to look for him, but there was no sign that he had ever been there.

Walking slowly, Evren left the cave and made his way carefully down the cliff wall, his mind a torrent of confusion and questions. By the time he made it back to the camp, he still hadn't worked it out.

"Evren!" Amias and Padma rushed to him, and Carmo hurried to him a few steps behind his friends. "You're yourself again!"

Evren nodded and spoke quietly. "I'm a boy again, but I hope I'll never be who I was before. I've learned some humility since then. I learned what true beauty and wealth is, and it has nothing to do with money or good looks."

"I think we've all learned some hard lessons." Amias agreed. "Come, we have to tell you about Petia." He and his friends told Evren about the little girl, and Evren wept, going to her and holding her in a comforting embrace for a long while before letting her go.

It was a somber evening in the camp that night, and all the friends stayed close together and talked about realizations of the heart and shared the precious time they had together, knowing full well just how important it was.

Petia slept in Hanne's arms, and though Hanne tried her best to stay awake to watch her sister sleep, she finally dozed off herself. In the morning when they woke, they found that Petia was much worse than she had been the night before. The black web of poison had filled all of her veins and her body looked as if it had been shattered beneath her skin.

No one was interested in breakfast, so they packed up their camp and Cruz carried Petia as they made their way down the side of the mountain. Late in the afternoon Petia had grown terribly weak and asked Cruz to stop so she could sleep. The friends were all afraid and worried as they came to rest near the place where the fairies had been on their way up the mountain.

Cruz laid Petia in a thick, soft patch of grass on the side of a small hill surrounded by tall trees that danced in the breeze, shivering their leaves like ripples on water. Amias made a fire and cooked a meal for them, and Evren stood thoughtfully, looking at Petia as she lay on the grass with her sister sitting beside her.

"I wonder if the fairies can do anything. I know we aren't far from where the emerald pool and waterfall were. I'm going to go look for them and if I find them, I'll bring them back here." He said pensively. He left without another word and Hanne watched him go, calling out a quiet thanks to him.

The hobgoblin made a special stew of herbs for Petia and took it to her. She could barely open her eyes when he knelt beside her. "I've made a broth for ye. It might help ease yer pain. It will help ye rest."

"Thank you, Meesta Trumbows." She tried to give him a pained smile. Petia dutifully sipped at the broth, but after only a few swallows, she turned her head away and rested on her sister's lap. Hanne held her and stroked her hair, talking to her about all the wonderful times they had shared growing as sisters. The others were close by but gave the girls some space to be with one another.

Evren came back much later, his face twisted in consternation. "I can't find the pool or the waterfall. It's as if they never existed. There's no sign of them. I know they were around here. I know we're in the right place, but there's just nothing there anymore. I'm so sorry."

Hanne only sighed. "Thank you for trying."

The rest of them ate some of the meal, but Hanne wouldn't leave Petia's side or put her down at all; she continued to stay where they were on the soft grass, holding her sister in her arms.

Night fell around them and the fire in the camp glowed warmly just at the bottom of the little hill. Cruz slept by the fire, but the friends and Mr. Trumbles stayed on the hillside with Hanne and Petia. Evren covered the girls with Padma's peaceful dreams blanket and they stayed awake as long as they could but sleep finally took them all.

Hanne opened her eyes when the first morning light reached through the leaves and touched her. Her thoughts immediately went to Petia and she realized that her sister wasn't in her arms. Sitting up with a jolt, she looked all about and drew in a sharp breath.

"Petia!" She cried out. Her sister was gone, and there was no sign of her. Carmo, Padma, and Amias awoke, followed by Mr. Trumbles and Evren. They all looked about them, but the girl was nowhere to be seen.

"What is that?" Carmo asked, standing up and pointing to a row of mushrooms before him. His finger followed the row and he found himself turning in a circle.

Padma stood up and looked at the circle of mushrooms. "It's a fairy ring!"

Evren frowned. "I looked for the fairies last night and I couldn't find them."

"It looks like they found us." Mr. Trumbles said thoughtfully, looking at the ring.

Hanne jumped to her feet and turned in a circle, looking at the mushrooms. It had encircled all of them as they slept. "I don't care about the fairies, I want to know where my sister is! Do you think they took her?" She cried out desperately.

Just then a few warm lights appeared around the ring, and the children grew silent. One light, a small fairy, floated up toward Hanne. Hanne glared at it. "Where is my sister? What did you do with my sister!" She almost shouted as tears streamed down her face.

The little fairy flew slowly in a circle around Hanne and came to stop and hover not far from her face. Amias walked to Hanne's side and stared hard at the fairy. Taking Hanne's hand in his, he spoke quietly.

"I think… I think you're looking at your sister."

Hanne's mouth fell open in shock. "No… she's not a fairy! She…" Hanne couldn't say anything else. The brightly lit fairy flew before Amias' face and then sunk down to his hand holding Hanne's, and landed on their hands together.

Hanne and Amias stared at each other for a moment and then lifted their clasped hands as one, gazing at the little fairy perched on them.

Hanne blinked in amazement. "Petia?" She whispered. The little fairy twirled and blew a kiss to Hanne. Tears filled Hanne's eyes. "You're a fairy? But how? How did… how did this happen?"

Mr. Trumbles eyed the little fairy who was once Petia. "At a guess, I'd say the fairies transformed her last night just as she was about to depart this world, dear lass."

Hanne felt as if her heart had broken in two. "How can this be? How is it possible?"

"It's a blessing, it is. Petia's not gone, she's just transformed." Mr. Trumbles said quietly.

"Petia… if that's you, come home with me. Don't stay here." Hanne pleaded, her eyes locked on the bright little thing before her. The fairy rose from Hanne's and Amias' clasped hands and hovered near Hanne's face. In a delicate movement, the fairy leaned close and kissed Hanne's cheek, and then twinkled brightly before she flew to the other fairies that were hovering at the edge of the fairy ring.

"Petia no! Come back! You have to come back! I need you!" Hanne cried out to her, but the small cluster of lights swirled around each other and then rose up into the trees, through the foliage of leaves, and disappeared in the brilliant morning sunlight.

Hanne sank to her knees and buried her face in her hands, sobbing. Amias knelt and wrapped his arms around her, and Carmo joined them, as did Padma and Evren. They held each other for a long while until Hanne had run out of tears, and then Cruz came to them. They told him what happened, and he comforted Hanne.

"She is gone now, dear girl. The only thing to do is go back home to the village and tell your parents what's happened. Come along. We can't stay here." He helped the others pack up the camp and Padma and Evren held on to Hanne's hands as they made their way down the side of the mountain in silence.

Chapter Nine

Full Circles

The friends traveled down the mountain all the way to the river where Petia had tried to follow them and gotten hurt. Instead of crossing the bridge, they walked along the bank until they found a place where the water was shallow and a log had fallen over the width of it. It was far from their path, but none of them wanted to walk across the bridge Petia had fallen through.

They camped one more night and the next day they made it to the edge of the forest where Amias had joined them on their quest for the Wish Weaver. It was there that Mr. Trumbles stopped them.

"I shall be staying in the forest. The village is no place for me." He said with a half-smile, looking up at each of the friends. "It's been me pleasure to travel with ye, to know ye, and to call ye friends of mine. I wish ye all the best, and may ye find some peace, Hanne." Mr. Trumbles gave her a nod.

"Thank you, Mr. Trumbles for all that you did for us. You were such a help. We wouldn't have made it without you." Amias smiled at him.

"Well this doesn't have to be goodbye." Carmo grinned at the hobgoblin. "I think we can all meet here sometimes, just to visit and say hello, and I promise to bring pastries."

Light smiles stole over the faces of the friends. "Then we shall meet here again. I'll come on the day of the full moon each month."

"We'll be here." Evren gave his small friend a hearty hug. "Thank you."

They all bid him farewell, and before their eyes Mr. Trumbles practically vanished into the forest. Amias thought he saw the little man's hat bobbing in the thick of a bush for a moment, but then he blinked, and it was gone. There was no sign of him.

"Let's get home." Cruz told them, urging them forward. "It's been a long time since I saw home, and I know that all of your parents are probably desperately worried about you. Hanne, Amias and I will come home with you to talk with your parents."

Hanne nodded in silence and Evren and Carmo took her hands in theirs as they walked away from the forest.

They were passing by the river, nearly to the village, when Padma stopped in her tracks and stared at the river. "Oh my!" She gasped, holding her hand to her mouth. Amias went to her.

"What is it?" He asked worriedly, not sure that he could take any more.

She looked hard at the river and the river bank. "I saw this! I saw this in a vision! The Wish Weaver showed it to me. I saw a boy fall in the river here and a woman pulled him out and saved his life!"

Cruz stepped up beside Padma. "That happened a long time ago. The boy was Omid. He would have drowned if the woman hadn't saved him. She was here washing clothes for the village; she did it as work. He fell in just there where the sand bar drops off and the water gets deep. She saw him fall in and dove in to pull him out

~ 176 ~

again. She saved his life." Cruz furrowed his brow. "I wonder why the Wish Weaver showed you that."

Padma knew, as she stood there watching the water swirl and roll over the stones, coursing its way down the hill toward the village. "I know exactly why she showed me. Omid saved my life when I was little, from that wolf that attacked me. My wish was that I had never gone into the forest so that the attack never would have happened. I have always felt as though I owe him a debt that I cannot repay. It's weighed so heavily on me all of my life. I didn't want to owe him, but now I can see that my debt isn't to him; it isn't to be paid backward."

Carmo tilted his head in puzzlement. "What do you mean?"

Padma turned away from the river and looked at her friends. "He saved my life when he defeated the wolf that attacked me, though he came away from it with a scar." Tears began to form in her eyes. "I can see now... he could never repay the woman who saved him all those years ago until he saved me from the wolf. I can see now that the good we do is repaid by paying it forward to others, by serving others as best we can and by being generous and selfless to them, as others have been to us. The best way that I can repay him is to be thankful for what he gave to me; my life, my future, and to pay all the goodness I can forward to everyone in my own life. That's not a burden, it's a gift, and it took me until just this moment to realize it."

She wiped the tears away from her face and smiled, for the first time in years feeling the weight in her heart and in her mind lifted and gone. She felt free, and it was better than magic.

"You won't need to change much then, Padma. You are already a gift to all of us, but I'm glad that you've let go of the past." Amias gave her a smile and they turned to go to the village.

When they reached the center of the village, the friends hugged one another tightly and said goodbye, promising to meet up soon, and then they headed on their ways home. Cruz and Amias went with Hanne as they had promised to.

Carmo hurried to go and see his grandmother. When he got there, he was mildly surprised that his father wasn't home or in the bakery. He dashed up the stairs to see his grandmother, and when he opened the door of her room, he saw that she was sleeping. Not wanting to wake her but anxious to be with her, he crept to her side.

He sat on a stool beside her bed, watching her sleep. He hadn't realized that he would miss her so much. She opened her eyes slowly a few minutes later and blinked in surprise when she saw him.

"My precious boy! Where have you been?" She asked with a worried look in her eyes. "Are you all right?"

Carmo nodded. "I'm okay. I went to see the Wish Weaver. Where is father?"

His grandmother sighed heavily. "He was worried about you too. He went out to go and find you, and he's been gone looking every day. He won't be back until dark."

"I'm so sorry, Gran Saša. I did tell you where I was going." He tried to amend what he had done.

"You did, but you know that it was much too dangerous for you to go." His grandmother sighed sadly.

"How are you feeling Gran? I missed you so much." He had hoped that the Wish Weaver might have granted his wish after all and that his grandmother might be on the mend and perhaps even up and around, but she looked much worse than she had when he left.

"I'm not well my dear. My time has come to leave this world." She reached for his hand and he felt her delicate touch and knew then that the strength in her was gone.

"No Gran! I went to the Wish Weaver to ask her to give you a longer, healthier life!" Carmo pleaded, hoping that might make a difference somehow.

"I would have wished for you to stay here with me so that I could have all of my time left in this world with you. There's nothing more I could wish for than that." She gave him a half smile as her eyes moved over his face.

"You didn't get your wish and I didn't get my wish." He replied sadly. Tears flooded his eyes. "The Wish Weaver tried to tell me this… to show me that my wish was about what I wanted and not what you wanted. I shouldn't ever have gone. I should have stayed here with you. I can see that now."

With a heavy sigh, he looked down at his lap. "I should have spent every moment with you that I could have. Time is too precious to be lost. We must cherish what we have."

Gran Saša gave his fingers a gentle squeeze and he looked up into her eyes. "Don't be sorrowful my boy. No good can come of it. I have cherished every moment I've had with you, and I understand why you went."

"Forgive me Gran!" Carmo wept as his heart ached.

She spoke softly. "I forgive you, but it's more important that you forgive yourself before I leave."

"Don't leave Gran!" He begged her, closing his fingers around her hand.

She sighed softly and gave him a smile. "You are the light of my life. I love you my boy." With that, she closed her eyes and her last breath left her. Carmo stared at her as his whole world came to a halt.

"Gran! Gran Saša! No!" He closed his eyes tightly, squeezing out the tears that formed there, and dropped his head down onto the blankets over her, weeping a long while as he held her hand. He stayed with her until his father returned home that night.

* * *

Amias eyed the trap in his hands carefully as he set it, making sure that it was just right. He knew he'd have rabbits for Hanne's mother in no time. Just as he was standing up, he heard the scuff of footsteps against the ground and he turned to see who it might be.

Surprise flooded through him as his eyes took in the form of Nassim, the stranger who had come through the village and first told them all about the Wish Weaver. He was dressed just the same as he had been before, in his black clothes with his big black coat and his dark black hat pulled low over his face.

Amias went to the man, and Nassim stopped before him. "Good day, young one." The man said in his steady, strong voice.

"Nassim, I did not think that you would ever be back to this village again." Amias eyed him curiously.

"I am coming through to talk with you on my way to other places." Nassim answered mysteriously. "Tell me, did you make it to see the Wish Weaver?"

Amias nodded and knit his brow. "We did... my friends and I." He answered, and something stuck in his mind that wouldn't go away.

"Were your wishes granted?" The man asked, looking as if he already knew.

"No, but lessons were learned by us all." Amias told him. "Did you make it to the Wish Weaver too?" He asked, narrowing his eyes. He couldn't get the thought out of his mind, and he hadn't realized the fact of it until just that moment.

"I did go, but I found only the remnants of a curse that once was and the hoofprints of a unicorn who was no longer there." Nassim's dark eyes seemed to be deeper than the night sky above.

Amias tilted his head to one side. "Well that explains why I didn't see you when we were there. I freed all of the souls from the Wish Weaver's tapestry cloak, and when I did, you were not among them." He had finally given voice to the trouble in his mind, and Nassim had given him and answer for it.

Amias only had one other question that wouldn't leave him be. "What was your wish?"

Nassim studied him with a half-smile for a long moment before he answered. "That my princess, my love, be freed. Fare you well, always, Amias."

The man walked away then and Amias turned and watched him go, staring at his back in utter amazement. When the man was almost out of sight, a strange black cloud enveloped him, and a moment later there was a great black stallion where the man had been. A gleaming white unicorn cantered out of the trees then and joined the stallion, and together they galloped up into the forest covered Kamala mountains, standing in majestic silence between the heavens and the earth.

The End

Mrs. Perivale and the Blue Fire Crystal

By Dash Hoffman

CHAPTER ONE

In a prim and proper townhouse, neatly set back from a respectable street in the poshest end of the Notting Hill neighborhood of London, lived an older woman named Alice Perivale. Mrs. Perivale was widowed when her husband, the late Lieutenant General George Perivale, passed away bravely in a battle on a distant shore in the service of Her Majesty the Queen of England.

Alice had left their spacious country home after George had gone, as she felt that it was too empty. Their son Edward had gone off to Oxford and then become an important businessman in the Central Business District of London. He'd married and had his own child, and Alice saw them all on holidays and occasionally on odd weekends. She had only been able to stand the quietness of her large home for a short while before she determined that it would be much better if she lived closer to her family in London.

She purchased a lovely townhouse, and she settled into it with her six cats, and her butler Henderson. Henderson had vowed to remain in her service for the duration of her life. He felt that it was his duty, his obligation, and indeed his honor, to do so. He took excellent care of Alice and her six cats. Alice said more than once that Henderson was the glue that kept the household together, and he did his best to live up to that bar. From making certain that tea was always served promptly at four in the afternoon to ensuring that Mrs. Perivale took the right pills at just the right time every day, he was the clockwork that kept it all going.

She had recently brought home a fluffy orange kitten with big green eyes that she had found homeless and hungry in the park down the lane. Alice cleaned him up, fed him, and introduced him to the other older cats, naming him Oscar, and explaining to them that they were to take care of him; he was their new charge. Oscar was having a trying time learning to fit into his new place in the family, but each day he grew a bit more comfortable.

It had been a gray and rainy morning on the day everything changed, though at intermittent points the sun had made an effort to shine at the edges of the clouds, brightening them somewhat from behind. Alice was seated at the old wooden roll-top desk in her small library. Marlowe, the Abyssinian cat, was curled up on a red pillow cushion on a modest chair beside her, watching her through heavily lidded eyes, while he purred quietly.

Nearer to the fireplace, on a thick soft rug, lay three more cats. Tao, the Siamese, was resting so still that she could have been mistaken for the statue of a sphinx. Her sea blue eyes were closed, her breathing slow and deep, and her tail was wrapped around her carefully. She often meditated in such a way.

Not far from Tao sat Sophie. She was picturesque, as always, with her long white hair carefully groomed, her posture elegant, her manner poised, and her slender diamond studded collar fastened about neck. Her sky-blue eyes were set on Alice as she sat at the desk.

Lounging in a cushioned basket right beside Sophie was an old grey cat with black stripes streaking back from his bearded-looking whiskery face. The stripes varied in size, growing wider as they reached the middle of his body, wrapping around him. His hair was long and soft, and more white hairs now mingled with the grey than before. Montgomery was asleep, stretched out lazily and happily, facing the warmth coming off of the flames in the fireplace.

In the window was another cat. She was all black, and her fur gleamed like smooth satin in any light. Though she gazed coolly around the room now and then, her golden eyes were diverted more often to the street outside, watching the passersby and the rain as it fell from the sky, rolled down the buildings and streets, and splashed in the gutters when cars swept by. Jynx was fond of ignoring the other cats and taking in the world that existed just outside of their home, but with the arrival of the fuzzy orange kitten, that had changed. She'd taken him under her paw, and watched over him more than the other cats did.

Oscar poked his head in the door and looked around, his green eyes wide and his whiskers twitching as he sniffed the air. His fur was fluffy and unkempt, sticking out in nearly every direction. His gaze touched on Tao, Sophie, and Montgomery beside the fire, and on Jynx in the window, who turned her head and looked at him patiently, but he stopped when he saw Marlowe on the red cushion beside Alice.

He padded over slowly, watching all the while, and sat at the foot of the chair, looking up at Marlowe, whose attention was on Alice.

Alice reached her fingers to a dark cubby hole in the inner shelf of the desk, just beneath the slats of the roll-top, and pulled out a colored seashell. It was shaped like an open lady's fan, and its warm shades resembled a spring sunrise: a rosy blush at the base blended into peach and then to a soft, buttery yellow that faded into a smooth vanilla crème at the scalloped edges of the shell.

Oscar meowed at her. She smiled down at him, lowering the shell for him to examine. He sniffed at it tentatively as she spoke quietly to him. "My husband George gave this to me. He brought it to me from far away and he told me that

~ 186 ~

he kept the other half of it, knowing that the two halves would always make a whole, even when they were apart. We really were one, he and I. I guess we still are, and we'll always be."

She waited until Oscar was satisfied with his inspection of the seashell, and then she returned it to its place in the cubby box in her desk. With a wistful smile, Alice picked up her cell phone and cleared her throat as she swiped her finger over the screen to call the man whose photograph was smiling up at her from it. The phone at the other end of the line rang a few times.

"This is Edward Perivale." The man's voice came through deep and strong.

"Hello, Edward. It's Mother." she said happily. She was always glad to hear his voice; it brought his face directly to the forefront of her mind, along with many of the sweet memories she had of him.

"Hello, Mother. How are you doing?" he asked, sounding distracted.

She curled her fingers tighter around the phone. "I'm well, thank you darling. I was hoping we could have dinner soon. Perhaps tonight, if you're all free." She didn't want to use up any more of his work time than she had to, and got right to the point.

He sighed heavily. "Mother, this really is the worst time. Annabel has a meeting, Eddie is playing in a match, and I'm right in the middle of a deal at work that needs all of my attention."

Alice pursed her lips together, looking up from her desk to the window before her, watching as rivulets of raindrops rolled down the glass. "Well… perhaps I could go to Eddie's game. I'd love to see him play in a match."

"No, Mother, he's riding along with some of the other boys, and neither Annabel nor I will be going to this one. It's clear on the other side of the city. It wouldn't work for you to go." His tone was strained and weary.

With a deep breath, she set her shoulders back a little. "Is there another night soon when we could all have dinner together? I miss you all, and it would be lovely to see you. I really did move to the city just to be closer to you, and it seems like I don't see you much more now than I did when I lived in the country." Alice willed herself not to be dejected.

He breathed out a long sigh. "I have no idea. There's no night I can think of right now. Perhaps Annabel can look at the calendar and try to find a time. We'll have to figure it out later. I really do have to go. I'm quite busy at the moment."

Alice stared at the window, not seeing anything past the rain water washing all down the pane. "Of course. I'm sorry to have bothered you."

"Bye, Mother." Edward answered shortly, and hung up his phone.

Alice sat there in silence, holding the dead phone to her ear, and closed her eyes. Swallowing hard, she pushed down the emotion rising from her heart. With a shaky sigh, she set the phone back on the desk and lowered her hands into her lap, clasping one around the other.

Her hands were old and her skin pale, the darkness of her veins showing through here and there. Her fingers, once slender and pretty, were a bit more knobbly at the knuckles. There were delicate crepe paper lines where the skin had once been smooth. She began to lose herself in the years she could see on her hands.

The subtlest sound of a cleared throat pulled her from her reverie. Alice blinked and drew in a breath, turning in her

~ 188 ~

seat to look behind her. Henderson, her butler, was standing there. All of the cats were looking at him. At his feet was another cat that had followed him into the room. It was a very fat calico cat, whose fur was white with big splotches of orange and black all over, from his nose to the tip of his tail. His face was flat and had the slightest look of being pushed in, which only served to make his cheeks look wider and rounder. Bailey looked up at Henderson expectantly, watching him closely. Bailey was always hungry, and he had developed the habit of following Henderson around until he was fed, when it was close to mealtimes.

Henderson's coat was black, and the longer tails of it hung down at the back while the front was cut short at his waist. He wore a white button up shirt with a small tidy black tie, crisply set at his neck. What little hair he had left was combed over to one side, and his narrow body stood at attention. His lean face was turned up ever-so-slightly in sincere concern.

"Excuses me, Madam, I was coming in to ask about your evening meal tonight. I… couldn't help but overhear your conversation. I apologize, I hadn't intended to eavesdrop." He lifted his thin eyebrows a little.

She gave her head the merest shake. "Not to worry. It's fine, Henderson. I think I'd like beef tonight, and whatever Fran wants to make with it."

He nodded and turned to go, but stopped after a step and faced her once more. "Madam… if I may… as I understand it, there is a new group coming together at the little church beside the park, just down the lane. It's a Widows of War group. They are forming to help each other and to do service in the community where it's needed. I wonder if that might be of some interest to you. I have no doubt you'd be quite a helping hand to them, if you joined them. I think they're accepting new members until three this afternoon." He gave her a hopeful and encouraging smile.

Alice smiled back at him. "That sounds like a good group, Henderson. Thank you for mentioning it. I believe I'll go and have a look and talk with them. Perhaps there's something I can do for them. Maybe I could be of some use to them."

Henderson gave a slight nod and left the room with Bailey waddling close behind him, meowing at him. The cats shared looks amongst each other, and turned to gaze up at Alice. She rose from her chair and glanced down at the phone on the desk. "I guess since my son is too busy for me, I'll go see if this Widows of War group could use some help." She walked to the door and turned her attention down to Marlowe, who was right at her heels, where he always was.

"Marlowe, dear, it's raining. I doubt you'll want to go. You'll get wet." She spoke with a tender half-smile.

He looked up at her expectantly and pawed gently at her foot.

She sighed in resignation. "Very well then, you can come, but don't complain about your fur getting soaked. You won't let me put a raincoat on you, and the best I have is the umbrella. Sure you won't stay? No? Well, maybe you'll be all right." The corners of her mouth curved up a little more. "Come on then. Stubborn boy." She chuckled quietly and they walked to the front door together.

Alice pulled on her mismatched gloves and her brightly colored purple coat. She dressed well, but she couldn't deny the spice and sass that had flowed through her all of her life. Besides, she thought to herself as she set her matching purple hat decked out with ribbons and flowers atop her head, if the

~ 190 ~

Queen of England could go around dressed in every color and look wonderful, so could she.

Giving herself a peek in the mirror, she leaned in a little closer and considered her reflection, just as she had been considering her hands earlier. When she was younger, she'd had dark hair and fair skin, rosy cheeks and full lips. She'd been quite a belle. Time had drawn itself around her slowly and carefully etching every moment, happy and sad, good and difficult, into her face. There were smile lines framing her mouth, and laugh lines extending from the corners of her eyes. She had been happy for most of her life, and it showed. Her cheeks were fuller than they'd been in her youth, and the dark color in her short hair had faded to nearly all white, but her brown eyes were as warm and kind as they had always been, and she had a welcoming smile for anyone who took the time to look at her.

With a gentle tug on the edge of her hat and a nod of satisfaction, she picked up her umbrella cane with the bird's beak shaped handle, and reached for the door, holding it open as Marlowe lifted his tail and stepped out with her into the misty rain.

They walked side by side along the road. She was careful to avoid puddles so she didn't splash water onto Marlowe. He held his head up; his eyes wide as he looked all around them, his ears alert and pointed sharply. She held the umbrella over them both, though she wasn't sure just how much good it was at covering the cat beside her.

They had just rounded a bend in the road when Alice stopped short and gazed at a spot on the sidewalk opposite them. She peered closely and frowned. Marlowe stopped beside her, staring at the place where she was looking, and then turned his head up to her with curious eyes.

"Marlowe…" she began quietly, leaning her head slightly to the side as she spoke across her shoulder to him, "did you see anything over there… just now?" She blinked a few times and looked harder at the spot on the sidewalk. "I was certain I just saw some kind of little animal over there, but there's nothing there now. I could have sworn…" she trailed off and bit gently at her lower lip.

Alice finally took her eyes from the spot she was staring at and looked down at Marlowe, who tipped his face back up to her. "Did you see anything?" she asked again. He meowed and waited for her.

Drawing in a deep breath, she raised her brows and shook her head. "It must have been a trick of the light. Could have sworn I saw… something." Her eyes narrowed in puzzlement for another moment, but then she shrugged and began on her way again.

After a short walk, and carefully crossing one street when the cars had stopped, they made it to the church. It was a small building made of gray stone blocks and set with stained glass windows that had been in place since before Alice's grandmother had been born. A single narrow bell tower rose from one end of the church, housing an old brass bell that rung out on Sunday mornings.

Reaching for the worn door handle on the thick old oak door, Alice looked down at Marlowe. "Now, you won't be allowed in here. I'm sure they'd have a fit. Who knows if their church mice have claimed sanctuary, but you'll have to wait out here for me. I won't be long. I'm just going in to sign up for their group. I want you to stay right here by the door, and don't go off anywhere. I'll be back soon enough."

She looked straight down her nose at him and he meowed and sat at the side of the doorway, his eyes locked on her as he curled his tail around himself. There was a donation box above his head, and he was under it just far enough that he wasn't being rained on. Alice gave him one last serious look, and stepped into the church, closing the door behind her.

She walked into the small reception hall that was off to one side of the church, and as she entered through the doorway, she saw a small table where a young woman sat with a few stacks of papers and a cup filled with pens. The young woman had mousy brown hair that was pulled back into a sloppy bun, and a small mouth with thin lips that were pressed together in a hard line. She lifted her hazel eyes and looked over the top of the squared glasses that were perched on the end of her narrow upturned nose.

"Can I help you?" she asked in a cool tone.

Alice gave her a warm smile. "I hope so. I'm looking for the Widows of War group. I'd like to learn a little more about it and sign up for it. Is this where I-"

The young woman lowered her face in exasperation, giving herself a double chin as she did so. "Ma'am," she interrupted swiftly, "I don't really think there's anything that you could do for the group. It's designed for a younger crowd. I think you're just a little too old to try to do any of the things that we do in this group. We wouldn't want you to get hurt."

Taken aback, Alice stared at her and blinked. "Well, I realize I might not be quite as young as some of the ladies in the group, but I can certainly-"

The young woman cut her off again. "We just don't think it would be a good idea. We're only looking out for your best interests."

Alice gazed intently at her. "What is your name please?"

"Deborah." the young woman answered in a snappy tone.

~ 193 ~

"Well, Deborah, you keep mentioning this 'royal we' that you seem to be speaking for. Is there anyone else running the group with whom I might speak?" Alice was maintaining her decorum as best she could.

Deborah folded her hands and leaned toward Alice. "There is, but she's not here right now, and I do speak for the group."

Alice felt the rare flickers of annoyance and frustration ignite in her. "When might I be able to speak with this person?"

"Not anytime today." Deborah smirked with satisfaction. "By the way, I just thought I'd point out to you that your gloves are mismatched."

Glancing down at her hands, Alice turned them over as she inspected her gloves. "Yes, they are." She answered, looking back at the young woman before her. "I suspect one of the cats has gotten off with the mate to one of these gloves, or I might have left it in a pocket somewhere. At least I'm wearing them though, and at least I have manners."

Deborah stood up, her cool hazel eyes locked on Alice. "I don't think there's anything we can do for you here. I think you're just a little too old to be looking into anything like this. Perhaps you should focus on acting your age and doing things that people your age do."

Alice's mouth fell open slightly as she gasped. "And just what age would that be? How should I act? Should I stay in bed? Indoors? Should I just be done with my life since I'm so old? Well I've got a thing or two to say about that, Miss Deborah! I'm a long way off from the grave, and I have a lot of living yet to do. There is quite a bit that I could do for others, especially for the Widows of War group! I'm not about to stop doing anything that I *can* do, just because someone else thinks that I shouldn't!"

She was about to go on, but Deborah went to the door and stood beside it expectantly as she gestured for Alice to leave. "Thank you for coming in." Deborah said with a cold half smile. "It's raining. Perhaps you ought to go home, where you should be."

Alice clamped her mouth closed and walked briskly through the doorway. As she passed the young woman, she muttered, "You could do with a good dose of manners!"

Her chin was high and her fingers were closed tightly around the handle on her black bag as she pushed open the old oak door of the church and stepped into the fresh afternoon air. The rain had stopped, though it was only a brief break. Marlowe was sitting just where she left him. He meowed, his brown and gold eyes steady on her.

"Well, that didn't go well at all." She snapped in irritation as she planted her umbrella cane on the ground and began to walk. "Let's find a little spot. I need a few moments to gather myself."

Marlowe and Alice walked away from the church and down a pathway that meandered into a park. After a few turns, they came to a bench beneath a tree that looked as if it was a mostly dry spot. Alice sat and placed her bag on the bench, and Marlowe leapt up gracefully to sit beside her.

Blinking back hot tears, she patted Marlowe on the head and opened her bag to dig around in it. "I guess I'm not much use to anyone anymore." She sniffed as she pulled out a dime-store romance novel and set it beside her purse, going back into the depths of the bag.

"I used to do so much. I was really active and involved with so many things." She sniffed again and pulled out a butterscotch candy, setting it on her lap before reaching her fingers into the purse again. "That wretched woman in the church practically told me my life is at an end. She said they have no use for me. Perhaps she's right..." She trailed off and finally pulled a neatly folded cloth handkerchief from her bag before she pushed the romance novel back into the folds of it. She clutched the cloth in her hand and brought it to her eyes and nose.

"Maybe there is nothing more I can give to my fellow man. My son and his family have so little time for me, and now the Widows of War group doesn't want me. I just feel so useless! I can't give anyone anything if they won't let me, can I Marlowe?" she asked in a thin voice as she swallowed her emotion and rubbed her fingertips over his head.

He moved closer to her, purring and nuzzling his face into her hand as she petted him. With a weak smile, she tilted her head and her voice softened. "Thank goodness I have you and all the other cats, and Henderson. I don't know what on earth I'd do without all of you."

The two of them shared a long and quiet moment together, save for his loud purring. She opened her butterscotch candy and popped it into her mouth, rolling the wrapper between her gloved fingers. "She didn't like my gloves." Alice told Marlowe. "Just because they don't match. George bought one of these pairs of gloves for me when we were on our wedding anniversary holiday in Paris one summer. She didn't know that, did she? How could I toss away something as sweet as that just because it doesn't match? I was silly and I lost one of the gloves, but I still want to wear them, so I just wear a different glove on the other hand. It's not as though I'm ever going to get another anniversary gift from George again. I think short-sighted people can't appreciate the beauty and true value in things they don't understand. Last time I saw him, I was wearing this glove... he held my hand and kissed my cheek just before he left. Wearing it, I can almost feel him holding my hand again. I'm not about to give that up."

Marlowe listened carefully and watched her, and she rubbed his head again. "Oh dear... it looks like the rain is going to start back up. We should probably head for home, my darling." She tucked her handkerchief back into her purse and pushed herself up from the bench, taking a few steps toward a nearby rubbish bin, where she dropped the candy wrapper. She was about to walk away, but then she stopped short again, staring intently at the trunk of a nearby tree.

"Marlowe," she whispered, "I swear I just saw something over by that tree... that one, just there. Do you see anything? Is there a little animal over there? I'm so certain I saw one just now... not much bigger than you, but now there's nothing there at all! Look carefully, do you see anything?"

He peered closely along with her, and a low growl sounded from him. She gave him a nod. "That's what I thought. I can't be seeing things. I refuse to go senile. It's just that... there's nothing there now."

Alice frowned and harrumphed softly. "My goodness. Perhaps it's time to be getting back. Tea time soon." She opened her umbrella and glanced toward the elegant Abyssinian beside her. "Come along then, Marlowe. Let's get home." She straightened her coat and hat, and they set off together.

CHAPTER TWO

The gears in the massive old grandfather clock began to whir and grind, and the deep tones rang out from it four times as Alice spread her napkin over her lap. The cats were lined up at their dishes, and Henderson gave them each a bit of warm milk and a few treats before he came to the table and served tea and scones with clotted cream and raspberry jam to Alice.

"How did it go at the church?" he asked with a hopeful smile.

She furrowed her brow some. "Not very well. I don't suppose I'll be joining the group. They are looking for a younger contingency."

He looked genuinely disappointed. "I'm so sorry to hear that, Madam. Perhaps there is another group that might need your help elsewhere."

"Perhaps so, Henderson. Thank you." She gave him a little smile, wishing with all of her heart that it was true. "It is a great feeling for one to realize that they are needed." She added, lifting her teacup for a sip.

"It is indeed." Henderson answered pleasantly. "It's quite fulfilling." He spoke as if it were the one thing in his life that made him happiest.

When tea was finished, she rose from the table and sighed, feeling the weight of the world on her shoulders. "I think I'll skip the evening meal tonight, Henderson." She told him quietly.

He frowned slightly. "Are you feeling all right? Can I get you anything?"

"No thank you. I'm just a little tired." She said goodnight to him, went to her bedroom, and readied herself for bed.

Once she was in her nightgown, she sat in her chair beside the fireplace in her room, reading a book for a while as the cats all napped nearby. She tried to keep her mind off of the worries of the day. When the grandfather clock chimed eight times, she put the book down, turned off the lamp, and got into her bed.

Reading had not distracted her much from her thoughts, though she had tried to push them away as best she could. Deborah's cold words had cut at her and she wasn't sure whether or not they were true, even though she felt as though they shouldn't be. She didn't feel old. She still saw the world around her with the eyes of a woman less than half her age. That didn't necessarily mean that her body would let her do what her heart and mind wanted to do. She was still in decent shape, and strong enough, but her age had slowed her down a little at least physically, much to her disappointment.

She lay in bed in the dark, pondering over all the things on her mind. The shadows and light from the dying fire danced lambent across the ebony ceiling and walls, and she stared at them, watching them and listening to the ticking of the clock. Marlowe lay curled at her feet; the warmth from his body comforting her through the blankets on her bed.

He moved slowly and carefully, a few steps at a time, and she wondered at the edge of her thoughts what he was doing, as he rarely came up further on her bed than his favorite spot at her feet.

It was then that she realized Marlowe hadn't moved; he was still curled up by her ankles, his soft form and body heat against her, but his purring had stopped. Alice's breath caught silently in her chest as she realized that something else was taking very slow steps up the other side of her body, toward her arm.

She knew it wasn't one of the other cats. They never got up on the bed; any of them. They each had their own beds around the fireplace, and Marlowe had made it clear that Alice's bed was his, and nobody else was allowed there. He'd have had them off of it in a moment if it had been one of the other cats.

Her heart began to beat faster and blood rushed through her, pulsing in her ears as the slight pressure of the moving thing inched closer. Her eyes were locked on the ceiling, motionless as her thoughts shifted abruptly to the moment she was in. Her mind was focused with laser beam intensity on her predicament and somehow, somewhere in the vast reaches of her brain, an untapped strength took over, and she found herself feeling level headed and in complete control.

Whatever it was that was creeping up beside her kept pausing and then inching forward slowly. It stopped again. Alice waited until it began to move once more and then like a flash, her hand shot through the dark and she grabbed wildly at where she was sure the thing was.

Her fingers closed tightly over something very soft; a kind of silky fur, and just as they did, there was a loud squeak. A moment later, Marlowe was at her elbow, opposite whatever it was that she had a hold of, growling deeply as he stared at Alice's hand.

The softness inside her grip wriggled about, but she held on tightly as she reached over Marlowe's head with her free hand and flipped on the lamp beside her bed. Blinking in the light and pushing herself up, she saw that all of the cats were grouped together on the floor right beside her bed. She sat up as best she could and realized that she couldn't see what was in her hands. It looked as if she was holding on to thin air, except that where her hand was supposed to be, it wasn't. There was just nothing there to see, but whatever the thing

~ 200 ~

was, she had a death grip on it and it wasn't going anywhere, though it squirmed and pulled to get away.

Marlowe growled even louder and in a blink all six of the other cats leapt up onto the bed, surrounding Alice's body as she pulled the soft invisible thing onto her lap and gave it a shake.

"All right now, I've got you and I'm not letting go. You come out right this minute! Do you hear me? Come out! I don't know why I can't see you, but I know you're there and I've had enough of this foolish nonsense! Now *out!*" she demanded.

All of the cats and Alice watched in disbelief as color and form began to show through a strange looking fringe just before their eyes. It was as if a feathery curtain was parting, revealing the creature behind it.

Two big, dark, round shining eyes appeared; they were deep black, almost as if they were portholes to the universe. Around them was a thin sliver of an ocean blue ring which held varying shades of dark to lighter blue. The eyes were framed with extremely short light brown fur, and above each eye there was a delicately arched fringy antenna in place of its eyebrow.

Just below its eyes sat a tiny nose that looked like it could have been a cat nose, over a small mouth that was similar to a cat mouth, though wider, and shaped with an upward curve, so that it looked as if the creature was smiling a little. It might have been smiling, Alice wasn't sure.

The rest of the creature emerged then, and Alice realized that the feathery fringe that had been covering and hiding it was actually its tail. It was fanned out like a peacock tail, but it was all directed forward and was made of several wide, fluffy feathers that resembled ostrich feathers. There were shorter feathers at the base of its tail that were dark brown, and then longer feathers that reached up to the creature's shoulders and those feathers were a golden sandy color, but the longest feathers; the ones that draped all the way over the front of its body, were vanilla colored. There was no definite line of demarcation, the colors blended softly into each other where they changed.

The tail came up around the creature like a bubble, covering all of it and making it disappear, until the thing pulled its tail back, opening the feathers like a curtain, revealing itself, and then the little animal retracted all of the feathers and curled its tail into a nautilus spiral reaching up its back and resting snuggly just behind its neck, similar to a squirrel.

Its ears were perked up at attention, pointed and alert, and resembled the furry ears of a fox. It had small paws with four fingers and what looked like a thumb, as well as toes on its feet, almost like a raccoon. Alice could see that it had retractable claws like a cat, though the claws weren't extended. The fingers on its paws were shaded dark brown with white and tan spots on them. Though it had four paws, it stood upright on its hind legs.

The creature had a thick soft white tuft of fur in a V shape at its throat, which wrapped around to the back of its neck, similar to a bandana. The rest of its fur was varying shades of natural browns, from tan to mahogany, and black, and all of the fur on its body, save for the white fur neck collar, was short and silky, like a rabbit.

Its face had the shortest fur on its body; not even a quarter of an inch long, and Alice could see dark freckles of varying sizes and shapes all over the creature's face, almost as if it had been splattered with paint.

The thing stood at about a foot and a half tall, but it was cowered down somewhat, making height a little difficult for

Alice to determine. Its body was almost like a teddy bear shape with a gently rounded and protruding belly, but it didn't seem fat; rather that some of the roundness was an illusion of its fur, not unlike the cats encircling them, except for Bailey the calico, who was more belly than fur.

It blinked and a quiet chirping sound issued from its throat, though its mouth didn't open. Marlowe arched his back and vaulted up on his toes, every hair on his body standing straight on end, his eyes filled with fire, as he pulled his mouth back and hissed and spat, growling again dangerously.

Alice and the creature she was holding by the arm both looked at him in surprise, though Alice wasn't afraid, the creature was terrified. It whimpered and began to wriggle in her iron grasp again.

"Marlowe! Now hold on! We don't know what this thing is yet. Let's figure this out. Please, try to calm down a little!" Alice told him gently.

Marlowe wasn't listening. His body remained rigid and he stayed where he was, ready to pounce in an instant. Alice picked up her reading glasses from the nightstand beside her and pushed them onto her nose, tilting her head back and looking through them at the creature in her hand, as she shook her head almost imperceptibly.

"Well my goodness..." she spoke in a near whisper, but then her voice became sharp and strong. "I knew I wasn't seeing things today, you dodgy little ankle biter!" She dragged the thing a little closer toward her on her lap, glaring hotly at it. "What in the world are you up to?"

It reached its front paws up and closed them gently over her hand. "Had to see if 'et 'es you! I know 'et 'es you." He spoke in a light voice not much bigger than he was, with a strange accent.

Alice's eyes widened as she blinked at it. She hadn't been expecting an answer from him. She spoke to her cats all the time, but they never spoke back to her. The cats all scowled at it, except for Marlowe, who was still on the razor's edge of a full on attack. "Well of course I'm me! What are *you*?!"

He held his paws around her hand still, and she could feel their softness on her skin. His voice was a little clearer, though still light in sound. "I 'es Chippa. Chippa Mari. I 'es an Inkling."

Her whole face contorted as she frowned at him and looked at him a bit closer. "You're a what?"

"I 'es an Inkling." he answered, slowly beginning to pet his paw over her hand with a calming touch. "You 'es surprised by me?"

She narrowed her eyes at him. "Of course I'm surprised by you! I've never seen anything like you, but that doesn't mean you're getting off scot free! You've been following me today and I want to know what's going on! What do you want, Chippa Mari?"

Marlowe growled long and low again and Oscar the kitten slowly padded up the side of Alice's leg, his eyes wide and his orange fur fluffed out more than it usually was. He got just close enough to the Inkling's tail to lean out and sniff it carefully.

Chippa Mari glanced back at him nervously, and then turned his attention back to Alice. "Had to come. Had to find you. Have come a long way from home. From Mari Village."

"I've never heard of Mari Village." Alice said shortly.

The Inkling shrugged a little. "No… you wouldn't. Mari Village 'es very far away."

"Why are you looking for me?" she pressed, eyeing him suspiciously.

His eyes grew wider, though that didn't seem possible to Alice, and he continued to gently pet her hand with his paw. "Mari tribe need your help. Need you to come to Mari Village." He pleaded, "Mari tribe 'es desp'ruht!"

"Well that's certainly true if they think they need me." Alice muttered under her breath. "What do you need me for? Isn't there someone else who can help you?"

He shook his head and the soft fringe on the antennae over his eyes swayed with the movement. "No one else. Only you! We 'es in trouble! There 'es danger. Everything 'en danger."

"I don't need danger in my life." Alice said sternly, but she softened a moment later. "Why are you in trouble?"

He stopped petting her hand and looked at her in desperation. "There 'es the crystal was stolen from Mari Village, Blue Fire Crystal. Must be found. Must be brought back."

She frowned sharply. "The Blue Fire Crystal." She shook her head. "Well, I think that's just about enough of that. I'm not going anywhere with some strange creature to-"

"Inkling... I 'es an Ink-"

"-to God knows where in the middle of the blessed night. It's bedtime, just look at that, it's a quarter after eight already, and any reasonable person should be off to sleep! Now out you go! You've caused enough trouble for one day. Off with you, and don't let me catch you sneaking around here again!" She released him and sat back against her pillows, giving him an unrelenting glare.

His big black eyes shone with the beginnings of tears. "Please! You must come! Mari need you! Can't be anyone but you... 'ef I doesn't bring you back... I've failed again. Everything 'es lost." He sat his little body down on her lap and began to wring his paws as he looked down and sniffed.

"Please come!" he raised his eyes to her again, his paws holding tightly to each other, his soft pointed ears directed at her, and his big black eyes locked on her.

Alice felt her heart melt and she sighed heavily. "I don't even know where this place is that you want me to go to. You're some strange creature-"

"I 'es an Inkli-"

"-from some strange village I've never heard of.... Goodness knows where. How far away is it?" She couldn't believe she was considering it, but there was something about his tone and about him altogether that intrigued her.

"'Es not far for you." He answered in a soft voice.

"So this Blue Fire Crystal is missing. What do you need me to do about it?" She lifted her chin some and eyed him pointedly.

"We 'es needing you to come and help us find 'et." He answered hopefully.

She was quiet a moment, crossing her arms over her chest as she regarded him. "How do I even know that what you're telling me is true?" she asked, peering at him curiously.

He blinked and pulled his head back a little. "I 'es here, right 'en front of you. I doesn't think you 'es ever seen anything like me before."

"Well I saw plenty of you today." she snapped back at him. "You'd better come up with something more than that. Some kind of proof."

He sat down, fidgeting a moment and his feet curled and uncurled as he considered what she said thoughtfully. Reaching his paws up underneath the long white fur at his neck, he tugged and a small cloth pouch came into view. It was on a drawstring around his neck. He slid it open and his eyes danced a little as he reached in and pulled out what looked like a fiery twig. It shimmered and glowed like the embers in the fireplace just across the room.

Alice stared at it. "What is that?"

Chippa Mari smiled brightly and his pointed ears perked up as he held it up to her. "Thes 'es Tinder Root. Mari eat 'et. Inklings love Tinder Root. Comes from base of Flame trees."

Alice reached her finger toward it, and he pulled it away and wagged his other paw at her. "You shouldn't touch. Might burn you."

She stopped and gaped at him. "You're going to eat that?"

He turned his attention to the glowing root in his hand, and a wide smile came over his little face as his eyelids lowered and he gazed adoringly at it. "Yes. Mari love Tinder Root. Hot and spicy." He popped it into his mouth and the chirping sound came from his throat again as he closed his eyes and savored it for a long moment before swallowing it.

Chippa Mari seemed to come back to himself then, opening his deep dark eyes as he stood back up and took a few steps toward Alice, still on her lap. "Please... you have to come. Mari need your help! None 'es can survive 'ef you doesn't come and find the crystal."

Alice sighed and shook her head. Crossing her arms over her chest again, she turned her eyes toward Marlowe, who was still standing at rigid attention beside her, glaring hotly at Chippa Mari.

"Oh, Marlowe. He's certainly the strangest thing I've ever seen, but he does seem to be telling us the truth. I'll be honest, I hate to think of anything happening to him and to his little Inkling village. You know I can't stand to see anything suffer. Obviously. I do have seven cats." Marlowe briefly glanced at her before shifting his eyes straight back over to the Inkling.

Alice looked back at him. "All right, little Chippa Mari. I suppose I will come with you."

He was about to speak when Marlowe took a few steps closer, pressing his body against Alice's arm. Alice gave him a glance and then turned her eyes back to the small creature. "It looks like Marlowe will be coming with me. I should've guessed that."

Chippa Mari frowned a little, looking over at Marlowe. "...um, 'et 'esn't a good idea 'ef 'thes cat comes-"

Marlowe growled deep and loudly, bristling sharply again, his eyes piercing the Inkling.

"Oh!" he squeaked, "Okay yes, 'es fine, I guess." Chippa Mari nodded humbly, folding his paws together and frowning.

All six of the other cats on the bed began to walk toward Alice, looking from the Inkling to her. "Actually it looks like they all want to come. I didn't expect that. I hope that's all right."

The little creature looked doubtful, and shook his head. "Not good. I doesn't think they should-" he paused, looking around at them staring at him. "...uh... 'es going to make a lot harder to... um..." He shrank down slightly under their hard eyes and grew quiet. "'Es fine. I guess. Have to think of some way to explain to-" he stopped himself and looked up at Alice, giving her what looked like a pained smile.

"When should we go?" she asked him in an even tone.

"Now. Have to go right now." he answered anxiously.

She nodded. "All right. There is one question I have for you, Chippa Mari. How do you disappear like you do?"

He smiled a little, holding his paws together as he looked up at her with his wide, round eyes. "You can call me

Chippa. Mari 'es tribe name, so we all share name Mari, because we all one tribe, but you can call me Chippa."

He lifted his tail out of the nautilus spiral that it was in as it laid against his back, reaching to his neck, and he carefully fanned out all of the delicate fringed feathers, waving them almost like a fan as he turned to one side.

"All Inklings having tail like 'thes. When we 'es born 'et's small and wild, like rooster tail, but we grow and older get, tails grow bigger, softer, more beautiful. We 'es 'en danger, or we need to hide, then cover ourselves 'weth tail completely, like chameleon. Hides us so we blend 'weth everything around us, and we can't be seen. We 'es staying there, but can't be seen 'et all." He covered himself with his tail, arching it over his head and all the way down the front of him, until the feathers touched the blanket in front of his toes, and he looked as if he were in a feather bubble for a moment, but then he disappeared.

He lifted his tail and reappeared a moment later, smiling up at Alice. She raised one eyebrow at him. "You use it when you're in danger or when you need to hide?" she asked with suspicion.

"Yes." Chippa nodded and smiled.

"Or when you want to be sneaky." she added, giving him a meaningful look.

The tips of his ears dropped slightly and he looked down at his paws. "Yes. Sometimes then, also."

"All right, Chippa, you said we need to leave right away. I'll just get dressed and gather a few things, and tell Henderson that we're going. I want you to stay right here until I come back for you and the cats." Her tone was serious.

He gave her a nod and moved off of her lap so she could get up. The cats moved in closer to him in a circle, all of them watching him closely. Chippa didn't move as he gazed around at them nervously.

Oscar reached out one little orange paw to bat at the fringy feathers of Chippa's tail, and Chippa pulled his tail in close to his body as Jynx gave Oscar a stern look. Oscar pulled his paw back and sat with all of them as they waited.

Alice dressed and then went from one side of the room to the other, to the bathroom, back into the bedroom, down the hall, and back into the bedroom again, all the while stuffing various things into her ever widening black bag.

Finally she waved at the cats and Chippa and told them to follow her downstairs. The group of them went into the kitchen, where Henderson was putting clean teacups away. He looked over his shoulder at Alice and his mouth fell open. "Madam! What are you dressed for? Certainly you aren't going anywhere at this hour! Are you all right?" he worried over her.

"I'm fine, Henderson, thank you. I'm going out. I don't know how long I'll be gone." she answered simply.

He gaped at her. "What, in the middle of the night? So late? Where are you going?"

Alice stepped aside and Chippa came out from behind her; his little paws held to his mouth as he looked up shyly at Henderson, who stood nearly two feet taller than Alice. Henderson gasped loudly.

"What in... -oh my goodness!" he fumbled with the teacup in his hand, and then looked over at Alice. "Shall I call animal control at once?" he asked, setting the cup down and starting for the old phone on the wall.

Alice held her hand up and shook her head. "No, thank you, Henderson. This is Chippa. He's an Inkling, so he tells me."

Henderson blinked hard. "He... -he *speaks*?!" he asked in exasperation. He stared at Chippa for a long minute and then looked back at Alice. "Madam, I must insist. You cannot go."

Chippa drew in a breath and turned his big eyes to Alice. "But... but Messus Perf... Pel... Peliv..." he stammered worriedly.

Alice leaned down closer to him. "Perivale. Pear-ih-vahl." she sounded out for him.

"Pevi..." he tried again and shook his head, looking miserably ashamed. "I 'es sorry. Can't say it. I has trouble 'weth big words."

"Can you say Alice?" she asked kindly.

Before Chippa could utter a sound, Henderson stood straight up and gave Chippa a sharp look. "Madam, that won't do at all!"

Alice sighed and glanced from Henderson back to Chippa. "Henderson's very proper, my dear, there's no getting around that. Try saying Mrs. P."

Henderson balked, completely affronted.

Chippa wrung his paws a little and gave it a try. "Messus P." He brightened up and smiled widely when he realized he had gotten it right.

"Well that's-" Henderson began with a horrified look, but Alice held out her hand and stopped him.

"That's perfectly fine, Henderson. He can call me Mrs. P." She gave them both a smile. "Now, let's go."

Henderson grew greatly flustered. "You're going out? With that... -with... -where are you going?" his voice rang with panic.

"I think I'm going to Mari Village." Alice answered thoughtfully.

"A village? A vil... -there aren't any villages around here!" He scanned the kitchen with wide eyes. "You certainly can't go anywhere like that alone! I'll have to come with you, of course. I just need to pack a few-"

Chippa's mouth fell full open and his ears flattened to the back of his head as he narrowed his eyes angrily. "Heda... Henness... Hesson..." he was growing increasingly frustrated, "...now 'thes one has to come?" he finally shot out.

The cats and Alice all turned to him in shock. Chippa curled his little paws into fists and pushed them backward in defiance. "No! 'Thes 'es very many! Chippa came for one! One! Chippa came to get one, and Chippa had to say yes to all these others..." he waved his paw wildly at the cats around him, "and Chippa didn't want to, because Chippa already has explaining to do! Chippa says no! 'Thes one cannot come! Chippa cannot explain *all* of you! 'Es only supposed to be one! 'Thes 'es... -'thes 'es many more than one!"

He was shouting, at least as much as his light voice could let him, and his natural tone didn't lend itself easily to his frustration.

Henderson was flying around the kitchen, shoving several things into a black leather shoulder bag. He spoke in half-thoughts as he bustled about. "Tea... -medicine... - must have... -cat food! An umbrella... -heavens, I've forgotten the-" He dashed madly out of the kitchen.

Alice lifted her chin and sniffed. "He can come if he wants to. I don't care who you have to explain things to, he is with me, the cats are with me, and if you want me, you get them."

Chippa frowned deeply and glared. "Fine, but no more! 'Thes 'es all! Chippa already going to be 'en tr..." he stopped speaking and turned toward the door.

Alice followed behind him, and the cats trailed behind her. She picked up her umbrella cane and her black bag and opened the door for all of them. "Why are you referring to yourself that way when you talk? You didn't do that earlier."

"Chippa wasn't upset earlier. Chippa very upset now! 'Es how Chippa talks when he 'es upset!" he snapped, marching hotly down the stairs with his tail fanned out widely, shuddering behind him.

"Well Chippa, I'm sorry you're upset, but you'll need to hide yourself so no one will see you. It's dark, but still, if you're showing yourself, there's a chance someone might take notice of you. We probably don't want that to happen. You may be difficult to explain." Alice told him gently as they headed down the stairs to the sidewalk.

He stopped and touched his paw to his mouth thoughtfully. With a nod of understanding, he looked up at her. "'Thes will work." he answered, and faster than the blink of an eye, he had vanished. Where he had been standing, there was a paw print that glowed like the embers in the fireplace, and like the root he had eaten. It only glowed a dark orange and red for a moment on the sidewalk, and then it faded away.

Alice clapped her gloved hands together and giggled softly. "That's brilliant, Chippa! How do you do that?"

He parted his tail feathers just enough so that she could see his eyes and face and nothing else. "'Et 'es from Tinder Root. Warm paws when needs. Very warm. Follow me." He said quietly, and he vanished again. Glowing little paw prints appeared on the sidewalk behind him as he hurried along, and Alice and the cats followed them as the marks disappeared quickly.

Alice looked down at Marlowe at his place by her feet. "He must not be as mad as he was a bit ago. He stopped referring to himself in the third person." She chuckled softly.

They were nearly at the end of the lane when Henderson came rushing up the sidewalk behind them, calling out. His leather shoulder bag swung wildly against his back and his long black coattails flew in his wake, while he pinned his black bowler hat to his head with one hand as he hurried to catch up.

Huffing and puffing, he just made it to them as they crossed a quiet and empty street, and headed into the park where Alice had seen Chippa earlier that day. Chippa's glowing paw prints disappeared altogether when they reached the grass, so he lifted his tail and unveiled himself, waving his paw at them to follow him into a place where the trees were abundant.

Chippa paused before two trees that were growing apart from each other, but which were still close, and he reached his paw toward the trunk of one of them, running it gently along the bark of the tree in an upward motion. The tree began to bend slowly, leaning to one side as Chippa stroked his fingers in that direction, almost as if he was willing it to move, and the tree was doing his bidding.

When the tree had arced over at the top, Chippa went to the trunk of the other tree and did the same thing, only going the other way, so that when the second tree arced over at the top, it met with the first tree and created a natural archway.

When the branches and leaves at the tops of both trees had met and connected, he looked up at what he had created and chirped a moment. Chippa turned, his dark eyes shining at all of them standing behind him; Oscar, Tao, Jynx, Sophie,

Montgomery, Bailey (who was panting), and Marlowe, who was with Alice. Henderson was behind Alice, also panting.

With a shake of his head and a flip of his ears, Chippa waved his paw at them again to follow him, and the moment he passed through the archway of the trees, he disappeared. Alice, Henderson, and all of the cats stared at the spot where he had been. There was nothing there any longer; he had simply vanished into thin air.

Oscar padded forward and hesitated only a moment before bounding toward the archway, and a second later, he was gone, too. Jynx rushed into it right behind him, followed by Tao and Bailey. Montgomery looked over at Sophie and meowed to her. She wouldn't budge. Montgomery went to her, curling his body and tail around her, meowing once more as he stepped toward the place where the other cats had gone. She wouldn't move. He turned and followed the others, leaving Sophie with Alice.

Sophie looked up at Alice and cried, but Alice shook her head. "None of that now, Miss Sophie. Off you go with the rest of them. Come on."

Alice straightened her hat and she and Henderson, along with Marlowe, walked through the archway and disappeared. Sophie meowed again, going up to the area slowly, pawing at the air in front of her and crying.

A dog barked in the distance. Sophie looked in dismay over her shoulder for a moment, then leapt toward the archway and vanished.

To read the continuing adventures of Mrs. Perivale and many other exciting Dash Hoffman stories, please visit the official website:

www.got-moxie.com/bookshelf

Follow Dash!
Instagram @dashhoffmanbooks
Twitter @readdashhoffman
Facebook @DashHoffmanOfficial

Made in the USA
Middletown, DE
31 August 2020